THE
ORDER

Book Six of The Hayle Coven Destinies

PATTI LARSEN

ONE

Their laughter made me smile, the first time I'd felt like smiling in a long time, it seemed. Infectious, delicious, the exuberant excitement of a brother and sister at play without a care in the world.

If only. Though, for now it was easy for my son to forget his role in the end of the Universe as we knew it. As the Gateway, whatever that would ultimately mean for him and the rest of us, my son spent far too much time sad and quiet, doing his best to keep his chin up, his shoulders back. So much weight for a boy to carry, a weight I knew well and could do little to help him bear. I had my own burdens.

The last few days, though, felt different. Our takeover of the Gate cavern—a place I thought long lost to us with the death of my darling Liam—had given my children a refuge from the world, a space that welcomed us with intelligence and love. Shielded us from the outside in ways I could only be grateful for and refused to question. I now knew why this place remained despite Liam's loss. He'd stayed behind, left his soul here for us, in case we would need him again.

I dabbed at a tear in the corner of my eye and held still as Gabriel peeked around the edge of the bookcase in the Gate archive room, cheeks bright and flushed, hazel eyes sparking green. His tousled, blond curls glinted with red in the low light, reminding me with poignant hurt just how much I'd lost the day Fate took my husband away.

I envied them, Gabriel and Ethie, as his sister dashed from the darkness of a shadowed enclosure, leaping for her brother like a tiger ready to take down her prey. Gabriel snorted a giggle and spun, running back the way he'd come, into the endless distance of the stacks of the archive. I listened to the two of them howl their glee, my daughter's frowning face no longer a thundercloud of judgment and hurt. At least at the moment. Her anger at me would return, I had no doubt.

I'd earned it.

For now, I simply sat with Liam's computer in my lap, staring after them with my lips aching from the unaccustomed expression, wishing he was here to see.

And unable to let go of the possibility maybe—why was I torturing myself exactly?—just maybe, he might be able to. Magic was funny stuff, wasn't it? And hadn't I just discovered his soul remained behind here, or a piece of it, anyway, in the archive where he learned he was Gatekeeper to the Sidhe realm? Hadn't that dear, precious spirit connected me to Alison in the void, granting me answers I so desperately needed? In effect, saving me as he'd always tried so hard to do.

Wasn't it my turn to do the same for him?

Why had it taken me this long to realize Liam was exactly who I needed after all? I shivered at the thought of him, knowing how Quaid and I turned out, though my darling Sidhe Gatekeeper would never judge me. Things would have been so different, wouldn't they, if Liam had lived? No Gateway, for one. The Universe intact. Dark Brother without a way to cross from his side to this one, the threat of his powerful soldiers, The Order, vanished with the hurt and loss and death of the past... how long?

Dear elements, had it only been eight months since Zoe Helios crash landed in my back yard and signaled the end of my happily ever after?

I looked down at Liam's computer in my lap, slowly lifted the lid. This was torture, exquisite and demanding. I should have changed the image on the screensaver, should have erased it so I could focus on the task at hand instead of staring for endless amounts of time at the smiling, beautiful couple holding each other, barely twenty-one and fresh and, though they had gone through a great deal, so in love. Was I ever that young?

I traced one finger down Liam's cheek, smiling back at him, a soft splash of moisture landing and spreading over the keyboard. I wiped it away hastily, dashed at the tears on my cheeks, unbidden as always when it came to Liam. I'd fought so hard to keep inside all the hurt I'd gathered to me over the years. Being here, knowing how close he was to me, how near he had been... the frustration that I'd lost him again was almost unbearable.

I slammed shut the computer and set it aside, rising to the sound of my children's giggles in the distance. If there was any way to bring him out of the Gate space where his soul had resided I would find it. Selfish, of course. Not to save him, or not just to save him, but to have him by my side during the darkest time of my life.

I needed him, plain and simple. Anyone who told me he wasn't enough—strong enough, powerful enough— could go to hell and stay there.

Never mind Gram informed me the piece of him he'd left behind was burned up, gone. I'd believed her at the time. But being here the past few days, living in this space that felt so much like him, I was beginning to doubt her. And allowed maybe more hope than was healthy for my already shattered heart.

Whatever the truth, good or bad, I'd find it. Liam deserved the best from me.

My feet carried me out of the archive and into the passage, down the hall to the Gate room itself. Knees bending of their own accord, I sank to the ground, looking up at the stunning carved form of the route between my world and the Sidhe realm. How simple it seemed to me now, though at the time of its discovery I was in awe of the power of the Gate. But over a decade of regular travel through the veil between worlds— including time spent as a drach—had left this place unremarkable in some ways.

And incredibly precious in others.

If what Gram said was true, that Liam was gone at last, so be it. I just couldn't bring myself to believe it. The fact he'd stayed at all, remaining stuck here for all this time, was a miracle. And I believed in miracles these days. I had to. They were the only things keeping me from crumpling to the floor and weeping in desperate loss.

There was no doubt in my mind I had bigger things to worry about than this. Giant, huge, Universe ending things. The practical part of me demanded I stand up, exit the Gate cavern's protective space and get the hell back to it already before the entirety of creation imploded on itself.

But.

This was Liam we were talking about. And true love had to come first. Didn't it? Without love, what was the use in saving the Universe at all?

I refused to regret Quaid or my marriage to him. We'd created Ethie, after all, our gorgeous if stubborn and distinctly Hayle daughter. Despite our differences I still had fond memories of the quiet time we'd managed, that short and delightfully dull eight years between one disaster and the next. But it was clearer to me now than ever before the magic my mother and Batsheva Moromond embedded in us as infants was the only thing that held us together all that time. Severing it as I did left me empty and sad, but relieved, too.

Free. I liked freedom. I had so little of it.

Liam's loss gnawed at me as I let my mind wander. Not for the first time I reached out with my power, seeking him again. His touch was the most familiar thing in the world, should have been easy to locate for my not-inconsiderable magic. I had the strength of the Universe behind me it seemed at times and yet, tears returning as failure won, I clenched my teeth against the frustration of my inability to find one lost, dear soul. Refusing to believe, at last, Gram had been right.

Refusing.

I exhaled finally, angry, sorrowful, turning my face from the Gate. My gaze dropped, eyes falling to the black ribbon wound around my wrist. It twitched, sympathetic, the end stirring to stroke my skin.

"Help me," I whispered to it. "Please, I ask so little. Help me find him."

It tried, I'll give it that. It joined its power to mine, enough the suspicion I had about its origins added an extra layer of surety. Its power felt different, more like sorcery than drach magic. Max's supposition it came from the Dark Universe seemed to be correct, though it had never once threatened or tried to harm me. To the contrary. It had saved me a few times so far, including two ill-conceived attempts to reach the vampires in the void space between the edges of the veil.

The slender, pulsing ribbon of the drach soul I wore tried its best yet again, as it had since the moment Andre Dumont's dying vengeance against his former ally landed this treasure in my possession. I wondered at times what Liander Belaisle, the previous leader of the Brotherhood and now pawn of Dark Brother in our Universe, would have accomplished with the ribbon in his grasp. I'd never know. To take possession, he'd have to pry it from my cold, dead wrist.

Despite its attempt, and mine, our joined power twining through and around the magic of the Gate, diving deeply into the magic that created the barrier between my world and the Sidhe, we found nothing. Not a scrap, a hint, a breath of Liam. At last the ribbon settled on my skin and sighed.

I stroked it gently, sadly. "Thank you."

It twitched in its own frustration before falling still.

Another failure. But I wasn't giving up. Not on Liam, not ever again. There was a way and I would find it. Because he would never have given up on me.

I didn't have time to further beat myself to an internal pulp of regret and guilt. Not when the air of the chamber whispered behind me and an accustomed power touched mine.

Anger rose against her as I felt my jaw tighten on its own in response to her arrival. The last time I'd seen her she'd betrayed me. I didn't get up, didn't even look at her as Fate waited for my attention.

"Zoe," I said, voice rough. "I was wondering when you'd show up."

TWO

Now, don't take my tone the wrong way. Part of me was happy to see Zoe Helios, the new Fate on our plane. She'd saved my coven from the Brotherhood with her fiery warning back before my life went to hell. And I liked her, I really did. More so when she was just an Oracle, mind you. This new Zoe was a pain in my ass, to be honest. But the fact she was here, in the Gate cavern, could mean answers I was dying for.

Or more riddles from Creator via the Helios girl's mouth. We'd see which I was about to endure.

Angry and suspicious? Who, me?

"It's good to see you here, Syd," Zoe said, as if she'd been here all along and hadn't just met me eight months ago. It was weird to remember she'd been watching me her whole life, had once been convinced by her grandmother and Liander Belaisle I was the bad guy.

How much of my life did she really know about? I'd never had the chance to ask. And, frankly, I didn't care at the moment.

I turned slowly, looked up at her. It was easy to forget she was barely twenty, that her fresh face and dark brown eyes, olive skin and flowing brown hair meant one so young in physical form. She radiated power, especially now, Creator's Fate her master. Even when we'd met, the night she'd become the Phoenix—I still had to find out what that meant, added it to my tiresome list of After The Disaster stuff to remember to ask—she'd been a force to reckon with. One I was grateful to have on my side.

And had been all along. Until she and Trill Zornov paired up to betray me and hand over the foot of Creator's statue to my mortal enemy.

Friends like that, who needed a nemesis?

She must have known where my head was, because she sighed and shrugged, apologetic without being soft. "There is so much beyond your knowledge," she said, Creator's multilayered voice whispering out over Zoe's words. "Things you can't know yet, Syd. I beg you, do what you do best and trust I have the rest well in hand."

Couldn't argue with the maker of everything. Then again... when had I ever taken anything on face value, even from the Creator of the Universe?

"Whatever," I said, turning away again, irritation piqued, fully aware it was probably a terrible idea to treat

Creator and her Fate like they were pissing me off but far too broken and world weary to give a crap. "What do you want, Zoe?"

Her soft footfalls announced her motion, the sigh of her clothing and movement from the corner of my eye telling me she wasn't going anywhere any time soon. She folded her legs beneath her, sitting beside me, hands in her lap. At least she didn't try to touch me. I don't think I could have handled any kind of offer of kindness or familiarity from her at the moment.

"While there are details of which you must remain ignorant," she said, voice soft and quavering slightly, as though Zoe disagreed with Creator's decision, "there are others you must now be aware of."

"Should I thank you for the dribs and drabs?" Okay, I was being unfair. And an idiot and all the terrible names I'd called myself over the years. But, damn it.

Just, damn it all.

"It's time for him to come to you." Zoe's hands twitched on her legs as my heart leaped from my chest and lay pounding on the ground at my feet. At least, that's what it felt like. Shocking to find it still inside me, beating away.

Liam. She had to mean Liam. I could have hugged her in that instant, forgiven her anything, but Zoe wasn't done.

"When you meet him," she said, the reality of what

she told me sinking in and killing off the joy in my soul, destroying yet again any hope I might have Liam was returning to me with those near incomprehensible words, "you will know him." Zoe's brown eyes glistened with tears. I barely heard her through the shattered shock of loss yet again. Wait, him? Who him? "You must trust him." Her arms rose, hands fluttering ineffectually a moment before she seemed to collapse inward, shoulders sagging. "He's not only vital to your fate but is exactly who you have been looking for."

That made zero sense and I was fully prepared to throttle her for more information. But before I could reach out and smack her a good one, she leaped to her feet and backed away.

I glared up at her through slitted eyes, hating her all over again. Yes, hate. Strong word, that. But with the residue of Liam's hope still clinging to me hate had a place to settle and grow.

"You suck," I snarled. "You just suck, Zoe. Creator. All of you, all of it." I drew a breath to pull in my rage, feeding on my anger, eating me up inside until I found myself on my feet, too, fists clenched at my side. "Unless you have specific, important and helpful things to tell me, you can get your scrawny Oracle ass out of my Gate cavern and keep your Fate freak show to yourself."

Zoe flinched from me, hands rising to form a barrier between us. Was I that scary, even to her? I couldn't hurt her. I knew that. She was Fate, for the element's sake. And Creator sometimes. But no, it wasn't physical harm she feared, was it? I could see it in her face at last, registered her despair, her hurt.

It was her heart I stabbed over and over with my words.

Well. So be it.

"There is an order," she whispered. "And you, despite your power, remain inside it with the rest of us."

More riddles, though oddly her words helped calm me. No help from her, not really. Okay then. Business as usual.

Zoe shook her head, hair swinging, face scrunched as if she wanted to say more. But even as her mouth opened to speak, a tear trickling down her cheek, she vanished. Creator's doing? Or her own? Didn't know. Tried not to care. Failed.

Yeah. I didn't do hate very well.

Unless your name was Liander Belaisle.

I sank back down to the cool stone floor, feeling it warm beneath me. Reflexively, needing to wipe away the memory of the last few minutes, I ran my palms briskly up and down my thighs, skin whispering over denim.

I needed a clear head and Zoe's visit wasn't exactly conducive. Sure, I'd take the time to ponder what she said when I was more settled, less pissed off. Maybe I'd talk to Sass about it, or Gram. Max, even. The drach leader's calm would help me sort out my feelings. I missed being drach at times like this, missed the absolute level and cool emotionless state I'd lived for six months while my drach heritage allowed me the rest I needed.

Thanks for the reminder. My demon's snarky prod was fed with fire of her own.

You know better than to take it personally, Shaylee snapped at her, the Sidhe princess inside me shouldering aside my demon's flames with a burst of green earth energy.

Syd, my vampire sent. *We need to talk about what Zoe just said.*

In a bit. I shrugged both shoulders, shaking off the anger, their internal dialogue, as much of my own stress as possible. I'd had an idea with Shaylee's defense, her earth power quivering through me and into the stone under me, travelling toward the Gate where it zinged in tiny sparks at the base of the carved, wooden structure between planes. *I want to try something first.*

The fate of the Universe is more important. My vampire sounded contrite even as she spoke and, instead of being angry, I found sadness replacing my rage.

I know, I sent in return, feeling the three souls inside me hug me as I sagged into sorrow. *But I need to know.*

They continued to support me when I tapped into the power of the Gate and called out to Cian. Funny it had never occurred to me before, not once, to try to talk to the Gate maker. I knew about him, had known for years, since meeting Liam and discovering the reason for the Gate. The fact the Seelie lord had divided his soul into pieces to create the Gates from this plane to the Sidhe realm meant his consciousness had to be in there somewhere. My son confirmed it when he left his own body and entered the veil through the Gate not so long ago.

And, if anyone could tell me where Liam was, if he still remained here, it would be the soul tied to the Gate, right?

Worth a shot.

The Gate flashed green as I called out to Cian, both in mental voice and with Shaylee's earth magic tied to my own. The family power had bonded with me despite my attempt to keep it free, and though I wasn't coven leader any longer it held on tight and did my bidding as though begging me to pay it attention. Guilt, my old friend, washed softly at the edges of my sadness while I reached for the soul inside the Gate.

Honestly, part of me thought it was a lost cause, that surely after all this time—all the passed centuries—the soul of Cian was too fractured to talk to me. Sure, I could see Gabriel reaching him, at least enough to sense him. But for Cian to speak? To appear and have a discussion? A long shot at best.

I scrambled to my feet in shock and new hope as a tall, golden haired Sidhe appeared before me, a mild look of surprise on his face. He wavered as if unstable before solidifying, looking down to examine his long fingered hands, arching eyebrows climbing to his sharp widow's peak as his clear, yellow eyes settled on me.

"Daughter of the Light," he said. "Doombringer." Cian's flowing gold robe quivered at the hem as he dropped his arms to his sides and smiled. "Love of the Gatekeeper. Well met."

THREE

I hugged myself a moment, not sure what to say or do, staring in shock and hurt at the sight of him. I hadn't expected the form before me to elicit such a response, hadn't even for a second considered what I was doing, who I was actually calling. Until now.

Cian looked around, not noticing or caring I was a bit of a mess, I guess, a soft and near reverent look on his stunning face.

"It has been a long time since anyone chose to address me directly." His gaze returned to me, the faint flicker of his image reminding me he wasn't here in body, only in spirit. "Thank you for this, Sydlynn Hayle."

It was only then, as he smiled again and green sparkles flashed in his eyes, I began to function once more, freed from what held my tongue still, my heart quiet and aching. He felt recognizable, of course he did, but more than that. I was acutely aware as I drew in his appearance and accepted it at last the O'Dane family had not only taken on an identical look from Gatekeeper to Gatekeeper, but that they had somehow either been created in Cian's image or had evolved that way.

He was Liam, only perfect. Utterly, stunningly, deliciously perfect.

"Forgive me," he said in Liam's voice made more dulcet, deeper and smoother, a river flowing softly over smooth stones in a dappled glade. "I forget human hearts feel more keenly than ours. You stare at me for good reason, do you not?" One hand rose again, sparks falling from fingertips to the floor in a cascade of green. "You see the one you lost in me."

I nodded, swallowed. Not often I was caught at a loss for words, but this was a doozy so I figured I'd earned a bit of stunned silence, thanks.

"The O'Dane family has served me well," he said, tucking both hands into the arms of his robe, the gesture reminding me of Max and helping somewhat to free me from the last of the stunned sorrow the sight of him woke in me. "The best of all the families I have adopted over the centuries." Oh. My. Swearword. That meant there were others out there, didn't it? I'd never thought of that, the idea not crossing my mind until this moment. There were more human/Sidhe Gatekeepers who looked like Cian.

Who looked like Liam.

But Cian was shaking his head as if he knew exactly what I was thinking. Maybe he did. Our power was still linked through Shaylee and the family magic, tied to the Gate to keep Cian here.

"Only the O'Danes also carried my bloodline," he said, dispelling the tightening in my chest, the near panic I felt at the thought. Why did it bother me so much, the idea there might be more Liam clones out there in the world? Because I just couldn't handle it.

What if they were jerks?

Worse, what if they weren't and I went looking and found Liam, or who I thought was Liam, and couldn't live with myself for needing him so much I would accept him in anyone?

Get a grip, Syd.

Relief flooded me and I sagged, my own arms dropping at last from the desperate clutch I had on myself. "Thank you," I managed to choke out. Cleared my throat. "Do you know why I called you?"

"I can guess," Cian said, with more kindness than I'd heard from any Sidhe before.

I beg your pardon, Shaylee muttered.

Sorry, I whispered back.

Cian's smile perked at the edges and his eyes sparkled yet again. But when he spoke it was to me, not his fallen princess. "I may no longer possess a mortal body as you know it," he said, "but I am well aware of what has happened these centuries. More so, my attention has been here, in this place, quite frequently. Since you and Liam met." A faint hint of amusement. Nice to know we'd given him something fun to do. "I am unashamed to tell you I wept at the loss of the most recent Gatekeeper," he said, sobering, voice dropping deeper. Unbidden tears, uncontrolled and painful, burned in my eyes as he went on. "Liam was dear to me, more dear than you know. Which is why I felt great relief and rejoiced when Gabriel was born." He knew my son's name. Not sure that was a good thing, though it made sense. Still, the way he said it had a hint of reverence to it. Cian had to know who Gabriel was. Why did that bother me? He went on while my mind spun. "Though I understood your reasons for removing the power of the Gate—and agreed with that decision—it is good to have you and the boy home again."

Home. This did feel like home, I had to admit. And his reference to "the boy" stilled my fears. I knew Gabriel was special and so did the Sidhe lord's soul before me. Did he feel the need to soften the edge of my unfounded and odd worry with such a casual reference? It worked. And made me wonder how much Cian had been altered by his role as the Gate maker. He acted like no Sidhe I'd ever met.

Ahem. Shaylee really needed to just get over it already.

Stop being a princess and pay attention, my demon growled.

Snort.

"May I see him?" Cian's hesitation made my guilt quirk again. Tentative and soft, hopeful.

"Of course." I paused before turning. "But I have to ask first. Liam?" My turn to hesitate and for my voice to crack. "He was here all this time."

Cian nodded, full lips pulling down into a sorrowful frown, even more stunning in his sadness. "I tried to free him, to send him on, but he refused to leave." His golden eyes held mine. "He insisted you would return, that you would need him again. And he was correct."

He was. "Did you know the future, Cian?"

He shook his head, golden hair tinted red swinging over the floor. "I did not," he said, "nor do I. Though, I can only believe he did."

Made sense. Fate took him away from me. That same Fate had to have warned him, told me I would need him one day. And trapped part of his soul here, alone and waiting.

I'd hated Fate before. This time, that feeling doubled.

"He held no regret," Cian said, cutting off my fury before it could devour me and send me in search of Zoe Helios. To throw my power at the partial statue of Creator and just shatter the crap out of Her once and for all. "If anything, he was joyful knowing he would be able to see you again. Do not belittle his decision—make no mistake, it was his, Sydlynn—by blaming others for what he knew he wanted to do."

Fine. Whatever. Grumble mumble.

Love took over. I allowed it.

"Cian." I cleared my throat again, finding it so hard to speak. "Is he gone at last?" I didn't want to know. Needed an answer. Begged him to remain quiet a moment longer so the possibility of Liam's return could live another heartbeat.

More sorrow in the Sidhe's face. "I'm sorry," he said, destroying the final shred of maybe in my heart. "I don't feel him here anymore." He paused, head tilting to one side, a faint frown puckering his perfect brow. "At least, not in the Gate."

Okay, there was hope again. I leaped on it. "Then where?"

Cian's gaze left mine, drifted over my shoulder. He smiled again, raised one hand to point past me. I spun, found my son watching us.

"In him," Cian said. "Gone to the new Gatekeeper." The tall soul of the Gate maker bowed deeply to Gabriel. My darling son, face calm and much older than his eight years, nodded his head back. "Gateway," Cian said with great reverence. "All of my efforts and sacrifice have come to fruition. I am most pleased with you."

I knew the power of the Gate went into my son. But

Liam's soul?

Gabriel approached slowly, his sister slinking out of the archive and down the hall, watching with huge, blue eyes. Grave, sad, but with the power of presence I'd felt in him only a few times, my son crossed to Cian and raised his hand. The two touched briefly, the Sidhe's image flaring with green fire.

"Thank you," my son said.

I wept, unable to stop myself, despite knowing seeing me cry would hurt my son. Cian seemed to understand, met my gaze again, his face shining with joy.

"There is one person who might be able to help you," he said. "To locate what remains of Liam O'Dane, if such a part of him yet exists." He nodded to my son one more time before his image flickered and began to fade. "Question closely the one who tasked me with this life. I am the Gate maker, but it was her power that I used to build them so long ago."

With that, he was gone, with a final wave for my son.

And a scrap of hope left for me.

Oh, dear, Shaylee sighed. *She's not going to like helping us.*

Too bad, my demon snarled.

Indeed, my vampire sent. *But which of us, I wonder, is going to hold Syd back when Queen Aoilainn decides being unhelpful is a good idea?*

How I hoped she'd give me a reason to do her harm.

That would have to wait. My son stared up at me, his

young face full of gravity and wisdom.

"Mom," he said. "I'm sorry to make you sad. But it's time you told me exactly what happened to my father."

FOUR

While sitting on the floor in the Gate room might have been an appropriate place to have the conversation, considering it was exactly where Liam died, I wasn't comfortable talking to my eight-year-old son about the loss of his father in that place.

Forget his sadness. Total selfishness on my part drove me to move with my cheeks wet from my tears. I took his hand in mine, Ethie tucking in against my other side, the two children I'd do anything for and who held the weight of the world thanks to their parentage walking with me into the archive.

Sassafras sat on the desk, waiting for us. How much had the silver Persian heard? Everything, I had no doubt. He'd become a permanent fixture in this place, abandoning the family for my little brood and the quiet and security of the cavern. Not out of any need to feel safe, I was sure, but because I'd promised him when I left again—and I would, I was sure of that—I'd take him with me wherever I ended up. The Stronghold, another plane, somewhere away from here. To a place that didn't remind me the people I loved would very soon grow old and die and leave me alone to live forever.

He still didn't trust me not to go without him, I guess.

Amber eyes blinked slowly at me while I took Liam's seat behind the heavy, wooden desk that had been one of his favorite places in the world. It was odd to see my children perch on the tall, plush cushioned chair across from me, piling into it together. That used to be my place, with Sass in my lap, the giant hound of the Wild Hunt, Galleytrot, stretched out at Liam's feet.

But Liam was long gone and now so was the black dog. No longer believing himself of use or able to care for my kids, Galleytrot had chosen to return to the Sidhe realm. In shame, at least to him. As much as I missed having him around—the kids, too—I knew he finally had the life he'd longed for with Erica Plower on the other side. She'd been allowed a light sentence, in my opinion, though the witches who agreed to give her to Gwynn ap Nudd didn't think so. For her crime of betraying all witches to the Brotherhood she'd become a hound herself. Because of that, the black dog turned man, Jared Runnel, had seemed content enough when he crossed over to the realm to be with her. And while Erica earned her punishment, I was pleased for both of them they had at least a modicum of a happy ending.

Nice to know someone did.

Gabriel cleared his throat while Sassafras leaped to the chair my son shared with his sister and stretched himself out across both their laps. Ethie stroked the soft, silver fur while the cat purred, her eyes still huge. It was likely she feared I'd ask her to leave. Being included was probably the most vitally important thing in her life. She was still so young, too, barely seven. But they were both old past their literal ages, had seen and endured more than any ordinary child. And they were Hayles.

They deserved to know everything.

I'd told them a little about Liam when the two of them had finally asked who Gabriel's real father was. I know it hurt Quaid at the time, but it was readily apparent to anyone who looked at my son and then at my ex-husband the likelihood Quaid was his father was slim to zilch. Ethie, on the other hand, was all me mixed with her father's strong jaw and eye shape, enough of me and him no one would mistake her for anyone but a Hayle.

But, I'd purposely left out things, glossed over certain details about Liam's death. Yes, they knew my first husband died, that Ameline Benoit had been the murderess. So odd, this life of ours. Ameline's echo was now gone and her soul, cleansed of the evil of her upbringing, now a kind and witty person I actually liked. And Gabriel greeted her when he met her again after all that time with gentleness and acceptance.

There were things I didn't think the kids needed to know. But today, I didn't leave anything out. Even when Sass spoke up, just a whisper of faintest protest.

You're sure? He didn't judge, wasn't even seeming to call me out. Just sad.

It's time, I sent. *They're asking. And they need to know everything.*

And so, choking up from time to time and doing my best to remain stoic no matter my churning emotions, I explained exactly what happened. From being forced to choose a husband by the coven by my twenty-first birthday, a task I forced into a yearlong process but finally completed by marrying Liam. Max's betrayal at the hand of Fate and Liam's death, the fact he had no witchy echo and was lost to us as a normal would be—or so I thought. Gabriel's absorption of the magic of the Gate. He gasped at that, then nodded, chewing his bottom lip as I went on. And, at last, to the final fight between myself and Ameline in the maji chamber below the vampire mansion, after almost self-destructing when I thought Gabriel was dead.

I wound down, staggering to a halt, not sure how to wrap up what I'd just shared. Some pithy statement, surely, a moral to the story. But nothing came to me, not a single offer of comfort or glamor to tie the bow on that particular chapter in my life.

Ethie's blue eyes brimmed with tears. "And then you married Daddy?"

I smiled at her, wiped at my own cheeks. "I did," I said. No need to tell her the only reason I did was due to the magic our mothers had bound us together with as babies. "And we had you, beautiful girl."

She beamed at me before hugging her brother, laying her head on his shoulder. "I'm sorry," she whispered to him. Ethie didn't often show empathy, so self-centered I wondered at times if she was too much a Hayle. Sure, she needed to be powerful and controlled, but the balance of emotion, of caring was what made a truly great leader. She banished all of those worries from my heart with that one gesture, those two words. And, with Sass's soft sigh and head butt for her, I realized he thought the same.

And remembered, as my son gathered his thoughts, visibly preparing to speak, there were things I needed to discuss with my demon cat and my grandmother, Ethpeal. Worries they had about my daughter turning out like her mother. Whatever that meant.

"I want to give it back." Gabriel's first words surprised me enough I lost my train of thought about my daughter and focused on him again.

"Give what back, sweets?" The Gate was fine, obviously.

He turned to look at me, hazel eyes wet, cheeks pink. "My father's magic, Mom. I'm the reason he's not here anymore."

As I stared into that grief, I had an epiphany. Fate and Max and Liam and death all spun around in my head as I realized the true reason my husband had to die. Not to challenge me, not to force me to marry Quaid. But so my son could be the Gateway.

"Gabriel," I said, weeping again but feeling my heart lighten. "You can't. There's no one to give it back to. And this way he'll always be with us. In you."

My son choked on a sob, hands clenching in his lap as his sister patted his arm with great kindness. I thought of Max, of the suffering I'd put him through, sent him a silent thank you for carrying the burden all this time. Had he known the true purpose for Liam's loss? Possibly, though he'd seemed as unprepared for Gabriel and his Gateway power as I was. To blindly follow Fate like that...

Could I do it after all? Could I commit, as Zoe asked me, to trust and just act? Could I afford not to?

Gabriel could have fought me. I would have, at his age. Did fight my fate, I seem to recall, younger than him. Instead, my son nodded sadly, wiping at his nose with the back of his hand before hugging his sister.

The touch of power in the Gate room drew me out, away from my kids, Sassafras sprawled in their combined laps, watching over them. I paused at the door to the archive, feeling the great drach lord down the hall waiting with a hint of impatience unlike him, but unable to drag myself away from the sweet scene of my children in a big, wooden chair with a silver Persian weighting down their legs.

"What was he like, Sassafras?" Gabriel's poignant question made me cry again.

"Sweet," Sass said. "Kind." He snorted, amber eyes looking up to meet mine. "Too sweet for your mother. She bullied him all the time."

That made me laugh and allowed me to walk away, knowing, as I always did, in what excellent paws my children were held.

Smartass cat, I sent.

Bully, he shot back.

My good humor—bless him for giving me something to laugh about—lasted about as long as my trip into the Gate room. The moment I looked up and into Max's eyes, I understood the time for reminiscing and tears was over. Action hero Syd, at your service.

"Tell me," I said as the drach lord and his slim companion, the *lóng*, Jiao, waited for me with grim faces and tense postures.

"I'm afraid it's bad news," Max said in his deep voice. "For some reason, the Universe is disintegrating faster than ever, and I have no idea why."

FIVE

I was hardly surprised when Sassafras appeared at my side a moment after Max finished speaking, and not in his normal Persian form, either. Ever since my white sorcery had clarified the transition between cat and human, Sass had been spending more and more time as a young man than a furry feline.

Correction. He chose that particular form—all lean handsome with dark eyes and hair, olive skin and a sardonic grin that was so Sassafras I could still see the demon in him—whenever Jiao came calling. And, if I were to allow myself to go there, I would ponder the looks the two exchanged on meeting, the way they stood close together every chance they had, how they seemed content sharing space and air in a way that made me want to giggle.

Mind you, Max's news was no giggling matter. But knowing something warm and possibly life changing for my oldest friend might be brewing with the *lóng* girl, it at least tempered the edges of yet another disaster.

My son took my hand on my other side, staring up at Max with fearlessness that never failed to shock me. So collected and determined for eight years old. Was I ever that wise? Who was I kidding? Still not there.

Might never make it, either.

"Max," my son said, "explain. What exactly is happening to the Universe?" That hint of command, the way his fingers squeezed mine—not for support but to give it—made my heart tremble. He was growing up so fast, becoming someone I barely knew and yet understood completely at the same time.

The drach leader shrugged his broad shoulders, faint scales appearing on his gray skin as his alternate form shifted. I could still see the dragon he was, as if occupying the same space, a gift I'd not lost despite choosing to separate myself from my own drachness. It was almost easier to spot the restless discomfort in the massive shape than it was in Max's smooth and calm human expression.

At least my son was learning stoic from the best.

"I've seen it with my own eyes," Max said, Jiao nodding briefly beside him, her dark eyes meeting mine with concern tightening the corners. My *lóng* friend rarely showed emotion, so I was even more worried now. We knew there were planes vanishing. I'd witnessed it, too, after Trill stole the hand of Creator from me, the people of that world disappearing before the entire place popped out of existence. Surely Max remembered. Why the sudden panic? "Multiple planes simply absorbed into the veil, one after another like a chain reaction." Okay, so that was different. I swallowed nervously, hand convulsive on my son's. He looked up at me with a faint smile.

Reassurance from a child. That was what I'd come to? Oh, Syd. He wasn't a child. Not anymore.

"At least now we know where the planes are disappearing to." True enough. Liam's soul allowed me the connection I needed to reach my old bestie, Alison Morgan, mean girl turned friend turned ghost turned who-knew-what vampirish thingie. She'd told me as my love's spirit burned up that she and the vampires were there, trapped in the place between the veil and nowhere, along with members of the Order, Dark Brother's terrifying army. As well as countless beings and planes all layered over each other. As if waiting... for what?

For Doombringer to make her choice?

"It's only been two days since Gabriel returned the brain of Creator," Max said, his smooth voice roughened just enough I felt his concern like a vibration in my bones. "Despite our success in regaining a third of her pieces, the disintegration of the Universe seems to be speeding up."

"So what's causing it?" I wanted to pace. It was my favorite thinking and stressing activity, but I couldn't bring myself to release Gabriel's hand. "The Order?" Shudder. No way had they broken into our Universe. We'd know, I was positive of that. They were just too massive a power force for us to miss their arrival. "Dark Brother?" No, he had to be in his own Universe, too, or everything would have gone to hell by now. The Order were bad enough. The memory of their marching approach to the Gateway my son opened in Creator's statue chamber was fresh and biting. But I would never, ever forget the looming terror of Dark Brother rushing toward me in the maji chamber all those years ago, the night Ameline forced Gabriel to open a way between Universes and almost let Creator's evil sibling through.

Never.

"I wouldn't count out Liander Belaisle," Sassafras snarled next to me. True, the former leader of the Brotherhood was Dark Brother's pawn. He also had possession of at least one—if not more—piece of Creator. Those pieces, even separate, had massive power. We suspected Jean Marc Dumont, the new power behind the Brotherhood, was using the arm of Creator to convert Steam Union sorcerers to his side. Could Belaisle somehow be altering the composition of the veil and planes with a piece or two of his own?

"While he is powerful and connected," Max said, "I doubt even he has the wherewithal to send whole planes into the void." He shook his big head, brow furrowing in a rare show of pique. "I fear what is happening is a more natural reaction to events we are no longer in control of."

Gabriel didn't comment. Like he'd expected this news, wasn't terribly worked up about it. I'd known my son had information he refused to share, knowledge outside ours. Seeing him react without anxiety somehow stirred more worry in me—at least for him—and equally calmed me.

That is, until I acknowledged the true reason for the destruction of everything could be right in the spot where I stood. I swallowed before speaking, almost choking on the renewed fear of what I said. "This could be me, you know." Amazing how liberating it was to speak it at last, a quiet, terrible terror I'd carried along the way, growing in size and strength despite not knowing really how massive it was until this moment. They all stared at me in confusion. "Doombringer." My throat twisted convulsively for the second time. "Maybe I'm doing something just by travelling in the veil." Okay, farfetched, but fear had a way of knotting me up when I thought it was my fault.

"I disagree." Max's brow smoothed, a soft smile on his lips. "There is something happening, Sydlynn, but I believe the task that makes you Doombringer will be much less subtle and unexplained."

I wasn't sure if I should be relieved or not, except I preferred decisive choices, so I'd take his reassurance and suck up my worry. For now. Besides, he was right, wasn't he? My past involvement in the disasters that made up my life wasn't exactly what anyone would describe as "subtle".

I could wait on the blame game. There was always later to wallow and tremble.

"We need to investigate." I finally released Gabriel and hugged him, stepping back as he joined Sassafras. Only then did I see my daughter watching, peeking her dark head out of the doorway to the archive. She pinked when she saw me, as if embarrassed to be caught eavesdropping, but I waved to her and she nodded, shoulders squaring.

Fearless as she saluted me with a small pentagram etched in the air before her, glowing blue a moment before it disappeared.

"Take the kids to Gram," I told Sass as my son joined the cat-turned-young man, both scowling at me. "No complaining out of the pair of you." I jabbed a finger at Sassafras. "You chose me. That means the kids, cat."

He bobbed a nod, frowning.

"And you." I poked my son in his forehead once. "I know you think you can help, and maybe you can, but until we find out what's going on I want you to stay with your sister. Okay?"

He nodded, too, though he looked about as happy as Sass did. Pair of frowning, irritated bratskis.

I'd accept being the focus of their annoyance if they were safe.

"I'll come with you." I suppose I shouldn't have been shocked at Jiao's offer and suppressed a quick grin when she crossed with languid seeming casualness to stand at Sass's side.

Suddenly he seemed a whole lot less surly. Go figure.

I offered a wave to my kids before stepping through the veil at Max's side, leaping out and straddling his thick neck as the drach leader took his natural shape and winged his way into the veil.

All of my magicks opened, senses wide and tingling, searching for answers I knew would not be forthcoming. No way would we have it easy. Since when? Yeah, like never. Still, if easy fell in my lap I'd probably doubt it and go around it three different ways before accepting maybe it was the truth just out of sheer stubbornness.

It helped to focus on the problem at hand, especially when I felt the thrum of Max's power beneath me. I'd given up my drachness, my ability to fly, when I'd chosen to return home, welcoming the girls in my head back into wakefulness and the weight of the problems of my world on my shoulders. I still missed the freedom, the quiet and patience and peace, of being drach.

One day. I'd be free. Or so I kept telling myself. Since when did I ever get a happy ending that lasted?

If Max knew where my thoughts were taking me he didn't comment, instead winging his way to join Mabel and a handful of his fellow drach who hovered in the veil, waiting for us. Mabel's power—my bloodline—embraced me with her cool gentleness, the vast magic of the drach held back, a pulse like the heartbeat of the Universe in her touch as she spoke.

Three more planes have vanished that we know of, she sent, her tone so calm she might as well have been ordering dinner. *I can feel the veil shrinking in my very bones.* That registered with fear. Mabel showing worry was like the Universe falling apart.

Ahem. *Touché.*

I was about to speak up myself, to ask stupid questions no one had answers for, when the veil beneath us shuddered and sighed. And, in that moment, while the walls around a plane collapsed inward and the people, places and things of that plane disappeared with a soft sucking sound into the void, I felt a terrible chill pass over my soul.

Despite knowing it was happening, despite seeing it occur once before, this felt so final, so contrived and not random, the precision of the loss so complete I had no doubt whatsoever we were witnessing the beginning of the end. Of everything.

SIX

Failure was a crushing boulder on someone who seemed to have all the power of the Universe at her disposal. Case in point. I hovered there, clinging to Max's neck with my hands and my magic, heart pounding, head spinning, wondering what the hell was the use of being this megawatt pawn of Creator when a second plane began to crumble.

Oh, *hell* no. Not this time, not on my watch when I had said magic burning in my veins, begging to be used. Except, thrashing around like a lunatic, not knowing what I was doing, would likely either get someone hurt or make matters worse.

What's an all-powerful girl to do?

My white sorcery reacted even as I bopped around in my head, getting in my own way while my three alter egos spluttered and thrashed and my sorcery burbled its confusion. The power that was Creator's ultimate design for magic in the Universe reacted calmly, taking firm hold of me and focusing all of my attention on the edge of the veil.

At least someone knows what she's doing, my vampire muttered.

That was reassuring. Not. Considering I already had a trio of extra voices rattling around in my noggin, I hardly needed another. But the white sorcery didn't speak, didn't even show a real personality outside of taking control and showing me what I needed to see.

There, on the edge of the collapsing veil surrounding the plane. A thread of power, shimmering with the white magic itself, a thin and shining shield from the gaping maw that was the void. I realized as I threw magic at the edge the void itself didn't exactly draw on power. Only that its absolute lack of anything created a vacuum, much as I'd been taught space was like.

That was weird to think about as my mind settled into calm determination while my magic fought to do its thing. Was space really the void itself, just called a different name by normals?

Maybe if I'd had more of a chance to think things through the end result of my attempt would have turned out differently. Or, perhaps if the drach in my company—specifically the one I rode—didn't gasp and grasp for me, jerking my magic free of the sparkling veil edge, I could have figured things out. But, regardless the reasoning, I found myself still attached to the collapsing plane when it was sucked into the void, but without the benefit of control.

I'd been here before, spun forward into the blackness that devoured everything, feeling my very soul being sucked into nothing. Only this time, instead of reaching for specifics, namely my vampire friends, I chose to cast a wide open net of awareness as I plunged head first into the black.

The void was a jumbled mess of planes and those sparkling edges now pale and drained but still keeping the worlds apart, at least allowing them to overlay in a confusing pile of spinning people and stuff. I blinked through the sudden weariness as my own magic was devoured. Past the wavering confusion of the overlapping planes. Glimpses came through, the giant forms of the Order swiping at me on the way by, Alison's startled face as I rushed past her.

And had a thought despite the fear and the uncertainty as I fell. Why those two races in particular? Yes, there were whole planes and their inhabitants in the void. But as far as I knew the vampires and the Order were the only two races who came alone, without a place to call home.

Lassitude washed over me, darkness closing in around the edges. I faintly felt Max in the distance, pulling me back, but he wasn't strong enough. I'd been here before, yes, but never come so deep so quickly, and knew as I blinked slowly into the depths that seemed to go on forever I was at an edge of my own. If I didn't find a way to turn around now, there would be no going back.

And there would be no Doombringer.

That snapped me out of the paralyzing draw on my magic, though I shuddered at the bone deep exhaustion making me limp. I didn't have breath to scream, power to fight, heart to win. Not the edge, then. Far past that. Into oblivion.

I barely felt the pinch on my right wrist, the sting of circulation cutting off, my body jerked upward, lifting free of the void. I rushed past the vampires again, the Order in their shining armor, through planes and layers and people, rushing as quickly as I'd fallen toward light at the other end where giant drach forms waited.

And gasped a massive breath, collapsing on Max's neck while the black ribbon around my wrist released its clamped grip so quickly I whimpered at the agony of returning blood flow.

The girls shrieked in my head, voices gaining volume while I managed to fill my lungs once, twice, three times. It took everything I had in me to cling to the drach beneath me and pant air into my body.

The ribbon flexed on my wrist before collapsing, shuddering as I'd shuddered inside the void, the power within it almost spent. It had saved me once again, the soul of the drach from the other Universe that perhaps I should never have trusted. And yet, it had done everything in its power since we'd met to make sure I survived.

Either it was on our side or Dark Brother needed me alive. I was grateful no matter the truth.

"Syd." Max's voice held terror, warbling with drach song. "What happened?"

I raised my hand about an inch and let it fall with a thump on his neck. Energy flowed back into me through him as he fed me from his own personal power. I could finally sit up, shaking fingers raking my hair back from my face where it had escaped my ponytail.

"I tried to stop it." How foolish I sounded, how arrogant. "The white sorcery, it showed me how." Well, not really, but it tried. And damn me if I didn't want to give it a go again at a later date when I was up to it. Of course I did. "But I wasn't ready and the void sucked me in." I stroked my fingers over the black ribbon. "They're all in there, Max. The planes, the people. The Order and our vampires."

He nodded, a puff of smoke escaping his nostrils while Mabel glared at me, diamond eyes glittering fury. "Don't," he said, "ever do that again."

There was a time I would have bristled at being told what to do. But even as I considered how I'd do things differently next time, I shivered and hugged myself.

"We'll talk about it," I said. "One thing is certain. The Universe is collapsing in on itself and if we can't find a way to stop it, everything is going to end up in there." Made me wonder then. I spoke the question out loud. "If Order soldiers are winding up in the void, does that mean the other Universe is collapsing at the same rate?"

"That would make sense," Max said, regaining some of his composure. He spun and winged me back toward my home plane, Mabel growling something I didn't catch before we left her. "Even with the separation, the Universe demands balance."

"That means whatever happens here happens there?" At least we weren't the only ones suffering. Made me feel a tiny little bit better.

"We will work on that assumption." Max backwinged and stopped at the edge of my plane's veil, heaving a huge sigh. "You frighten me so very much at times," he said, barely a whisper I caught thanks to the tie of his magic. "How you throw yourself into danger without thought or consideration. And yet," I didn't get a chance to defend myself despite my demon's grumbling, "without your courage and willingness to risk, we would be in the dark about much we now know and are beginning to understand." Max cut the veil and tossed me through, following in his human form. I landed on the floor of the Gate cavern, hugging myself as the drach lord crossed to me and embraced me. "I would ask you to be more careful, but I know you would ignore me. And that doing so might mean our downfall."

I squeezed him back, tears burning the corners of my eyes. I always felt so small next to him, even when I was a drach. Not that he lorded over me, never. Just that his vastness, the dragon shape of his natural form and the power of the first race hung around him like a tangible aura I couldn't help but be affected by.

I pulled away from him at last and wiped at my cheeks, the overtired reaction making me emotional. Yeah, I'd blame that for the tears on my face.

"As long as you're always there to catch me," I said, throat tight, "I know I'll never fall."

Max flinched slightly, shook his head, frowned. Then sighed and shrugged.

"Daughter of my heart," he said. "You honor and terrify me."

Fair enough.

I didn't get to prolong—or ruin—our squishy moment. Even as I opened my mouth to respond, a sharp prod of magic slammed into me and left me gasping. I knew that power, understood instantly it wasn't an attack, but my own energies reacted in defense mode even as Gram's voice roared in my head.

SYD! I was moving before she was done saying my name, tearing at the veil, latching onto the family magic through our connection, Max behind me, bless him. *HELP ME!*

I let my appearance be my response, bursting into the kitchen of my old house in Wilding Springs, weariness forgotten, powers blazing as I landed with a snarl and a ball of blue fire in one hand, orange in the other.

Whatever was bothering my grandmother wouldn't last another heartbeat.

And stuttered to a halt, mouth gaping, as Demetrius Strong, face sad but stern, stepped into a tunnel of black and disappeared, leaving my grandmother to collapse to her knees and sob like a child with a shattered heart.

Sassafras and Jiao struggled to hold her back as my demon cat in human form met my eyes, his full of grief.

The Brotherhood, he sent. *However they're doing it, however they are changing the power of the Steam Union, Demetrius is one of them, now.*

SEVEN

There was no time for me to freak out over the sorcerer's loss, not while my grandmother melted down in front of me. One of the strongest people in my life, Ethpeal Hayle had been through hell and brimstone and fire so many times she rivaled me in that regard. Through all of her trials and losses I'd never seen her lose her crap.

Until now.

"Gram." I reached for her with my body as well as my power, wrapping her up, trapping the desperate feel of her, the broken and horribly hurt pressure of her grief in as much padding as I could, squeezing her tight as Sassafras wiped continually at his face while he stood over us.

Gram's power tried to open tunnels, her sorcery still active despite the fact I'd reawaken her witch magic by forcing her to take on the family power when I'd left to be drach six months ago. Instinct drove her, perhaps, the link to her husband calling to her soul to use the magic that connected them. I rocked her and breathed and forced myself to hold her tight as gently as possible while she battered at me in frantic desperation.

LET ME GO. Rage replaced terror, a good sign. In my experience anger fed me and I was her granddaughter, after all.

Not until you calm down. Not fair of me to ask, not knowing what we did. With the use of the piece of Creator in his grasp Jean Marc Dumont had just poached Demetrius from the Steam Union and made him Brotherhood. Not after my grandmother spent decades first married to a man she didn't love then insane and finally finding her true soul mate once again only to have him ripped from her.

I knew how I'd react. And that made me the right person to keep her here. Because with every effort she made, I anticipated her move. We understood each other too well for her to escape me now.

Didn't keep her from trying, oh no. And she had some sneaky ways about her. But my power was just too vast. The horror at her loss distracted her enough by the time she collapsed, panting, her face reflected her utter dejection.

Don't you quit on me, I sent, soft but with an edge.

Then let me go. Gram twisted physically in my arms.

Not that way. Now she'd settled, my own anger burbled to the surface. I looked down into eyes as blue as my own, into a face beloved to me and ground my teeth together before speaking in a voice like tearing metal.

"It's time," I said, "to find Jean Marc Dumont and make him wish he'd never, ever heard of the Hayle family." Gram wept, hugged me, kissed my cheek. "We'll get him back, Gram." I helped her to her feet while my body ached with the need to act, to do something. Oh, I planned on it. And the moment I had that piece of wasted space in my possession, I wouldn't hold back.

About time, my demon growled. *And to hell with who sees the body.*

No hiding. No longer. The Dumont family had done enough damage. The moment had come to end their evil legacy once and for all.

I held Gram's hand, the only anchor that could keep me here and prevent me from flying off as she'd wanted to do in pursuit of Demetrius. Because there was nothing I could do to save him from what had happened. Or was there? The white sorcery inside me might have answers, but I was still tired from my journey into the void. And I'd rather recruit some assistance.

Syd. Max's sadness told me he was going to say something I didn't want to hear.

PRIORITIES. I shot that one word at him. *The Universe can wait, damn it.*

He hesitated before sighing in my head.

"I'm coming with you." Gram's voice vibrated with need, her eyes still wet, her entire body shaking from the strength it took her to stay in one place. I knew how she felt.

"No," I said so firmly she rocked back on her heels. "You're not." I glared over her shoulder at Sassafras who frowned back. "You are going to stay here," I snarled, "watch over the family," I gestured around me, "my kids," I caught a glimpse of the both of them watching with huge eyes and sorrowful faces from the entry to the hallway, "while I make Jean Marc and his little cult go away."

"You're not going alone." Sassafras sounded as bossy as ever, despite the fear in his voice. For me? No. Not for my safety, not that way. He was afraid I'd do something I'd never forgive myself for.

"Don't be an idiot." I didn't mean to snap at him but this was just too much. I couldn't think about Demetrius, his cherub face, his kind blue eyes. Refused to reflect on the way he loved my grandmother with all his heart and made her so happy she seemed at times to forget the horror of her past. Or the fact he'd taken his own long, wretched journey into pain and insanity, winning his freedom and his true love after what the Brotherhood had done to him. I wouldn't go there. Not until he was safe and back with us and Jean Marc was dead. "He might not like it much, but Piers Southway is about to get a visit." He still blamed me for the loss of his sorcerers, for leaving him like I did. Because it was all about Piers, the fact I shed the people I loved and lived with the drach for six months. Yeah, that was it. I left because of Piers, to snub him, to show him I didn't give a crap about him. Not because I was heartbroken and shattered and needed to heal.

And he called me self-centered.

"Hissy fit or not," I said, tearing open a hole in the veil, Max at my side to my surprise, "the leader of the Steam Union has a job to do."

I left my family there, knowing they would be safe, but that from this moment on nowhere in the Universe would be so for Jean Marc Dumont.

The castle in Scotland felt quiet, somber. Screw that. They could be as sad and mopey as they wanted, the Steam Union sorcerers and their blond leader. I pounded my power through the heavy stones of the sprawling building even as I reached out with my mental voice.

PIERS SOUTHWAY. Okay, so shouting was becoming a way of life for me. Best I could do under the circumstances. Beat shaking the crap out of the ground beneath my feet. Something Shaylee was more than happy to participate in if I decided such an act was warranted. I figured one of two things were likely. Either Piers would ignore me or he'd come running.

Ten black tunnels opened in the foyer of the castle and a horde of young sorcerers poured out, led by the tall, lean focus of my attention.

He looked tired, black circles under his gray eyes, his longcoat dirty in places, the white button up he usually wore open at the collar, showing the stark standout of his collarbone. Piers had lost weight, looked like crap.

Not my problem. "Jean Marc has Demetrius," I said without preamble.

Piers halted his advance, his people behind him. A terrible frown creased a deep line between his eyebrows, lips turned downward, aging him by decades. "I see," he said, voice crackling with anger. "So, when it's my people in general you don't give a damn. But when it's someone you care about?" He tossed his head, blond hair greasy and unkempt, so unlike him. "I call rubbish, Sydlynn Hayle."

I shrugged. "You can call anything you want," I snapped back. "If you're about done having your little hissy fit, I suggest we focus our attention on locating Jean Marc and the piece of Creator."

Piers barked a laugh. "What do you think we've been doing while you abandoned us?"

Asshole. He did not get to say that to me. "You know how much is at stake," I said, hating the vibration of emotion in my voice. "You were there when Zoe gave me the white sorcery, Piers. When she made me sever our

53

connection. Because of your mother." I may have gone too far with that little additive, but it was enough to make him flinch and back down, if only for a second.

I should have apologized. The irony of this entire conversation wasn't lost on me. After all, finding Jean Marc was a priority. He had a piece of Creator. But both Max and I decided knowing where a piece was meant less than hunting down the three that had yet to be located. We could find Jean Marc when we needed to, at least that was the supposition. But now? Top of the list.

"Good luck in your search." Piers sounded like he hoped I choked on it. "The Steam Union will proceed with our own investigation."

He turned, about to walk away. Oh, no he did *not*. I pinned him with power, knowing it would piss him off and possibly damage our relationship irreparably. But I had to make him listen. He was so far gone in his anger he reminded me too much of his mother, Eva. And I couldn't let that happen. All of my own rage dribbled away when he didn't fight back, just held his place, glaring.

I couldn't lose my friend to the madness that claimed his mother.

I told him about the elder council, about the ancient collection of races who had watched over the paranormals of this plane for millennia. Two familiar faces in the crowd seemed shocked by the revelation their grandmother was involved. At least Apollo and Owen Zornov didn't know their Nona was on that council. Made me feel a little better. They were my friends too and I'd hate to think they chose to keep things from me the way their grandmother and sister did. Thinking about Trill just made me angry all over again.

"So?" Piers seemed unimpressed, unmoved by the information.

"So," I said, "they have resources we don't. And are looking for Jean Marc right now." At least, so I'd been told. "I figured it was time to check in with them and see if they'd come up with anything." And no, I didn't trust them, not after the fiasco with Femke and my own mother. The elder council wasn't exactly in it for the benefit of others, it seemed to me. Still, if they could help, I'd take it.

With a grain of salt.

Piers hesitated. A good sign. He still wasn't fighting my grip, either, though he finally pushed gently against me, another positive indicator. At least, I'd take it as such. Wins were few and far between at times so I claimed what I could for the home team.

"Have you seen Zoe?" He swallowed after he spoke, as if regretting bringing her up.

I nodded, heart hurting for him, releasing him. Piers remained where he was, the anger draining from him, leaving behind pained resentment. Well, I'd take that, too.

"Just a little while ago." Was it only an hour or so? My life didn't waste time spiraling into insanity, did it? "She looks good, Piers. She's doing her job." I was defending the new Fate of this Universe after she'd betrayed me, really? But it seemed to help my friend. His shoulders sagged forward a bit, his face falling before his expression settled into forced calm.

"This council," he said, a spark of the old Piers showing in his eyes. "Will they be forthcoming?"

I shrugged. "Maybe," I said. "Maybe not. Figured you'd like to encourage them personally."

He nodded, hands flexing at his sides, a dangerous fury on his face before he settled into calm again.

"I accept your invitation," he said. "Let's go."

He didn't have to tell me twice. We might not be besties again, but when I opened the veil and stepped through, Piers's weighted desperation was gone.

And the wins just kept on coming.

EIGHT

I could have taken us right to the council chamber under the pyramids in Giza, but I was hoping to catch one of the members alone first. However, as soon as we stepped out into the bedchamber of the Empress of vampires I realized such a chance had been optimistic. At least Moa was in residence, the small, withered form of the first vampire perched on her throne at the foot of her bed. Her tiny, black eyes observed me as though she expected me and I wondered if she had spies in the Steam Union.

It was the tall, stunning Sidhe at her side that made me frown. Everonus, the criminal Fey left behind by Queen Aoilainn when she formed the realm and took her people from this plane observed me with his silver gaze, also unsurprised to see me.

But the third figure, huddled inside a colorful shawl,

did seem startled if only for a moment. So, perhaps the ancient two were better at hiding their shock than the little old maji woman who clutched at Moa's chair with one wrinkled hand. Nona looked away an instant after meeting my eyes.

Guilt? New or historic? I guess I'd find out.

"Doombringer." Moa's voice, so young and fresh, always seemed at odds with her mummified appearance.

"Cut the crap," I said. "We need to find Jean Marc Dumont and we need to find him now."

Piers twitched next to me, his impatience feeding mine. Though my magic had connected me to everyone I'd loved once, I'd severed those connections. Only Piers and I remained apart since I returned, on purpose. Perhaps on his side because of rage at me, but I hadn't forgotten the fact his mother was using our ties to each other to track me when I hunted the pieces of Creator. As much as I longed to renew our bond, I had to hold him at arm's length.

Didn't keep his power from bouncing off mine like a furious wasp.

Everonus shrugged elegantly. "We are otherwise occupied," he said while Moa hissed at him.

Great. More trouble. "Spill it." There was a time and a place for politocospeak and diplomacy. This wasn't it.

Moa looked away, her child sized body shuddering. "My people," she snarled, "in case you've forgotten, are disappearing." She spun back, glaring her anger. "I don't see you doing much to help, Doombringer."

Oh, no she did *not* drop that in my lap and expect me to take it. But it was Max who roared with all the power of the drach behind him, his rainbow magic shaking the entire castle. Moa meeped softly in protest, as if shocked by his reaction.

"Do not test us today," he said, booming voice carrying. "Or any day, child."

Considering she was ancient, that term had to sting. But Moa just sagged, a broken doll on an elaborate throne, while her *lóng* bodyguards stared at Max with tight expressions. Did they know yet they were the evolution of the drach? Surely Jiao had informed them. They seemed shaken by the power he'd displayed, though, enough I could see it in their normally blank faces.

"It's every race for themselves, is that it?" Piers's question startled me. I hadn't expected him to speak. He gestured at them with impotent rage. "I'd heard your elder council protected paranormals. Until push comes to shove."

Everonus scowled at him. "You have no idea—"

"Nor do I care." Piers cut him off with a growl. "All I see before me is a pathetic gathering of those who are unwilling to act. Who have always been unwilling to act." He turned toward me, power coiling under him in a black cloud that seethed with his anger. "We're wasting our time here."

I found myself reaching out for Sunny even as I nodded. And tried not to flinch internally when I couldn't reach my aunt. The vampire queen had returned to the mansion outside Wilding Springs, doing her best to protect the vampires who flocked to her side. She'd managed to save a few, but the power drawing them into the void wouldn't be denied forever. The fact I couldn't touch her mind with mine made me very, very nervous.

Until I felt the edge of shields, the push back from the spirit magic protecting the mansion. Okay then. Sunny had things in hand. Time to put this present problem to bed. Priorities. I'd be sick of that word shortly, I had a feeling.

"I fear the scourge is spreading." This time when Everonus spoke there was real fear replacing the inherent arrogance in his smooth voice. That didn't sound good. "Several of my Sidhe compatriots have gone missing."

Could they be in the void, too? It seemed likely, though I threw the question at Max anyway.

His mind sighed. *I fear that is the case*, he sent.

Not good at all. I made a mental note to check in with Mom and my sister, the Ruler of Demonicon, to see if any witches or demons were on the lost list. For now, focus, Syd. Focus.

At least the drach were all accounted for. I could have asked Piers about sorcerers, but he was losing his to the

Brotherhood, so the question was just bad timing.

Turned out Moa didn't have my sensitivity to my friend's losses.

"Are the sorcerers all accounted for?" There was a nasty edge to her voice that made me want to choke her. She knew exactly what she was doing and I had no doubt it was plain, petty bitterness at her own plight that drove her to hurt my friend.

"If you mean the ones not stolen by the Brotherhood," Piers snarled back, "then yes. As a matter of fact."

The old vampire's fangs showed as she smiled at him. "Then aren't you glad we've located Jean Marc for you?"

Piers's elation was sudden and tempered with greedy hunger. "Where?" Why did I have a sudden image of him ripping open the Brotherhood's new leader with his bare hands and drinking his blood?

Sorry, my demon sent. *My bad.*

I choked on a snort of laughter, my own heart lifting, before I clamped down on hope with a firm grip and crossed my arms over my chest.

"What's the catch, Moa?" There was always a catch.

But she shook her head, real fear replacing the cruelty of what she'd tried to do to Piers. Everonus shifted with discomfort, too, Nona bobbing a slow, steady nod in silence.

"No catch," the old maji woman said, surprising me.

She looked up and into my eyes with her fear naked on her face. "We need you, Doombringer. And we must trust you."

"Why?" They really didn't have to trust me. Never did before. In fact, they blamed me for a lot of things.

Nona sighed, deep and tired. "You came back," she said, barely a whisper. "You committed to this plane and to the Universe by returning and risking everything to do so." She smiled faintly, kindly, reminding me of Trill. "We must do what we can at this point to help you see this through."

Okay then. While I still didn't trust them in return, and doubted they gave me their 100% either, this was another win for the home team.

"Tell us where." Piers tensed beside me, hands clenched into fists that struck slow, steady blows to his thighs.

"You're not going to like it." Moa could have rubbed it in, but she sounded as weary as Nona.

"What else is new?" I snorted and dropped my arms to my sides. "Just tell us."

"In North America," Everonus said. "In the territory of the Hensley coven of California."

He said *what*? Tallah.

Oh. My. Swearword.

If Tallah was harboring the Brotherhood, I was going to kill her myself.

NINE

"How long have you known?" I was all ready to leap through the veil and end the Hensley coven, but oddly it was Piers who was the voice of calm reason.

He seemed more level, more balanced suddenly, the man I knew and cared about shining through at last. That helped cool my jets and bring me back to focus as Moa squiggled in her seat in discomfort.

"Does it matter now?" She gestured at me. "Go, fetch the piece from Jean Marc, return it to Creator and fulfill your destiny."

She did *not* get to give me orders.

Max shifted beside me, his growl and a puff of fragrant smoke all the evidence I needed he felt the same way. "Be careful where you tread, Moa," he said. "You have put this plane and this Universe at risk and I have allowed it. But the time for that kindness has passed."

She shrank into her throne slightly, though I had doubts she truly feared his wrath.

Piers shrugged at last, all the tension leaving him. Was it the ability to act that loosened his heart toward me? Or just the fact he finally decided working together was preferable to the uptight trio before us?

"Time to go," I said to him, ignoring the elder council members. "I get Tallah."

Piers's gray eyes were clear, even kind. "There are others who need to be in on this, Syd. And you know it."

What, the voice of reason suddenly? I wanted to smack him.

"I would think you'd be the last person who would want to wait." I didn't mean to grind my teeth at him, shocked when he chuckled then rubbed his tired face with one long fingered hand.

"Just take us to your mother already," he said, "before I change my mind."

We left the trio there to their ineffectualness and lack of action. Maybe something would snap in them, too. Wake them up, force them to do something. I wasn't holding my breath and, quite frankly, I trusted the two people in my company and their cooperation far more than I'd ever the elder council. Let them hum and haw and continue to conspire without doing a single freaking thing.

I had a job to do.

Mom looked up in surprise from her desk as I let us into her office. Damn, I should have warned her, but from the firm and determined look on her face, she already knew why we were there.

At least, the part about Gram.

I shouldn't have been surprised Varity was with her, the elder Rhodes Enforcer leader nodding to me all casual, as though this were another day at the office. Well, wasn't it? I was shocked to find my ex-husband in attendance, his black robe disguising his muscular body, the accustomed tang of his chocolatey spiced magic giving me a moment of sadness that startled me more than his presence.

Thankfully, Piers was there to take over when I hesitated, covering up my instant of old hurt as he plunged into what we'd just been told. Mom sank to her chair again, eyes huge when Piers told her about Tallah.

"What has she done?" Mom's jaw tightened while Quaid stood, grim and frustrated.

"I shouldn't be here," he said, shaking his head at Mom when she stood again, protest on her lips. "I want to help, Miriam, you know that." The man I'd once shared my life with shook slightly, visibly torn. "But you know I'm not allowed to interfere. Not without talking to Femke."

We all knew where that would end up. The leader of the World Paranormal Council had changed.

Understatement. She'd turned into a crazed and broken shell of the witch she'd once been thanks to the Russian Mafia leader who'd kidnapped her. We'd rescued her, sure. But she'd been beaten, drugged and under the influence of a Black Soul sorcerer. I'd tried to reach her, only to be told by the elder council the WPC was to remain ineffectual so they could do their job.

The realization at that moment I was finally able to act hit me like a blow. Quaid must have seen the shock and sudden joy on my face, because he paused, blue flames pulsing around him.

"You're going to help, then." Relief reached me, his and my own, mingled together.

Oh crap. Now I had two imminent things to deal with and both felt immensely important. Tallah? Or Femke? Kick ass or save a friend?

I had to even think about it?

"I'll see you in Hong Kong," I said, not kindly.

Visible calm altered his expression, loosened the tension there. He'd asked me not so long ago to act on Femke's behalf. I'd turned him down. I was so done disappointing the people in my life.

"Don't worry, kiddo," Varity drawled, winking at me. "I can handle the Hensley's and the Brotherhood. We'll keep you posted on tracking down Jean Marc through Tallah. If she knows where he is, if she's truly betrayed us, I'll know about it in short order."

Quaid nodded, looking more calm and himself than he had in a long time. When he disappeared into blue fire, I turned to Mom, decision made.

The elder council might not have given me much, but their unwillingness to share triggered my own need to be the exact opposite of them. And gave me a brilliant idea I might well come to regret.

Without asking permission, I strode forward and grasped my mother's hand, connecting with the woken sorcery at her base. She gasped in surprise, wide open to me as I thrust my white version at her and felt the darkness devour some of it.

When I pulled away, I feared I'd feel weaker than before. After all, I'd been drained just recently by the void, hadn't had time to fully recover and here I was giving away the ultimate magic of Creator. Instead, to my surprise, I felt stronger than ever and shivered with the icy pleasure that came from connecting to the fresh power in my mother's control.

She stared at me with wide eyes before hugging me in a suffocating grip. "Syd," she whispered.

"Yeah," I whispered back, hoarse as the magic bound us so tightly together I knew this bond would never be broken, not even in death.

"I didn't know you could do that." Mom released me, wiping at moisture standing in her blue eyes. The streaks of silver in her hair seemed reduced, the deep line that had shown her advancing age not so noticeable now. Renewed vigor seemed to glow from her cheeks, her eyes and her smile made me feel young again.

"Neither did I." I turned toward Varity, held out one hand. She accepted readily, moments later beaming at me as our own connection pulsed between us.

Piers was next, though he hesitated. "Mother," he said, that one word all he needed to say.

I shrugged. "Let her try to track us through power she doesn't have." At least, I hoped that was the case. Regardless, I was willing to take the chance. Piers needed what I could give him, needed the edge against the Brotherhood that would mean success. For I had zero doubt sharing had even crossed Jean Marc's mind.

In fact, I was counting on his greed.

Piers's alteration was the least apparent visually, but the most magically. I felt his power lighten, if that was possible, the white sorcery washing free the bits and pieces of his hurt while it pumped up his strength so much he glowed in my mind's eye for a moment before settling down again.

"Bollocks," he whispered. And winked.

But when I turned to share with Max he shook his head, smiling gently but sadly at me.

This is enough for now, he sent. *It's time to retrieve the piece, Sydlynn.*

Whatever his true reticence, I nodded and spun back

to the others, though I was sure the drach lord wouldn't be happy Femke was my issue of choice. He'd just have to deal with my decision to put her above Creator for the time being. I'd get to Jean Marc and his pesky pack of nastiness. And how.

Varity's lined face seemed younger, too, her grin cocky and brilliant. "Shall we?"

The veil responded instantly, though my first step was halted before I could make it when a desperate cry hit me hard and fast, as though Sunny only had an instant to send her plea.

SYD!

Her cry was all I needed. The veil diverted instantly, carrying us to the vampire mansion instead of Hong Kong, dragging Varity along with me by accident in my haste to help. I hurtled through, white sorcery ready. And stumbled to a halt, power failing, while the collapse of Sunny's shielding hit me like a blow.

I could only stare in horror as the hundreds of vampires filling the front yard of the mansion vanished in a wave of black.

Two figures remained behind, shuddering inside a crystalline structure of shielding. I threw white sorcery at Uncle Frank and Sunny, feeling them siphon it but knowing it was too late.

The void pulled at me, eager and hungry.

Syd. Sunny didn't sound afraid, just resigned but

confident. Her blue eyes locked on mine as the two wavered, shields failing despite my attempt to help. Did I hold back? Did fear keep me from giving them everything I could? I didn't want to consider that while the void sucked at the edges of my power, locked firmly on the two vampires I loved so much. *We will be waiting for you on the other side.*

And then, with a soft pop of darkness, they disappeared.

In that instant all of the spirit magic of our plane disappeared after them, the distant, desperate cry of the Empress of vampires going with it.

TEN

I ran. For Nepal and the spire castle and the soul of the oldest vampire in the plane. Not of my own accord. I'm a bit ashamed to admit it likely wouldn't have happened if I'd been left up to my own devices. But I wasn't given a choice.

My vampire persona took hold of me and threw me bodily through the veil and into Moa's bedchamber, déjà vu a momentary blip of disconcertment as I staggered to a halt at the sight of the slight, trembling vampire mother wavering as black fought to devour her.

Syd. Mom's voice sounded level in my head, but with an edge of fear I recognized as pure terror. *My spirit magic is gone.*

I know. I grit my teeth against my vampire's desperation while she reached for Moa and tried to hold her. I'd only ever once before felt the undead creation of

Iepa take full control of me, and was so surprised by her actions I let her.

But even she wasn't strong enough, not with all the power I had at my disposal, to hold Moa safe. The only thing that snapped me out of my complacency was the tug of the void, familiar by now, but stronger than ever as Moa cried out, hands outstretched toward me, vanishing into the black.

Pulling the vampire essence within me along with her.

Oh, *hell* no. My demon snarled her denial and latched onto my vampire, Shaylee grounding us deep within the mountain for support. I wrapped all of us in white sorcery, sweat leaping out onto my skin, body shaking as my vampire began to slip away.

No. Not today. Not on my watch and never if I could help it. I'd chosen to give up my drachness to save her once. I wasn't about to let her go now.

But the void, the pull, the power... so hard to resist, and my vampire was losing, I was losing. Until the black ribbon on my wrist, sleeping since our previous encounter with the darkness, snapped awake and, with an audible snarl, reached for Moa.

And in that instant, in probably the only act of selflessness she'd ever made, the Empress of the vampires cut the tie between herself and my vampire and pushed us free.

The void opening snapped shut. I stood there a long

moment, panting and trembling while the ribbon settled, its power still diminished but satisfaction radiating from it while my demon and Shaylee hugged my vampire close.

That, she sent, *was interesting.*

I snorted, a kneejerk reaction to the stress. *Understatements*, I sent. *Your favorite.*

She grunted and shrugged the girls off when we all realized she wasn't going anywhere. *It's quite possible*, she sent with sadness in her mental voice and touch, *I'm all that remains of spirit power on this plane.*

Max stepped through the still gaping hole in the veil and settled one hand on my shoulder. "In the Universe," he said, his own sorrow lingering. I felt his power, diminished and no longer a vivid rainbow. Even the drach were affected?

This was terrible news. We needed the strength of the first race to combat the Order if they somehow managed to break through. I had feared even before now Dark Brother's soldiers were stronger—at least in numbers—than Max's people. Now?

I didn't want to think about what might happen now. Not when this plane, this place where I'd always felt at home, suddenly seemed empty and dull. It took me a moment to realize the *lóng* had gathered, a dozen or so men and women, a pair of kids that had to be Jiao's brother and sister, staring at me without a trace of hope.

"Your time here is done." Max gestured at a new slice

he made in the veil, the Stronghold appearing on the other side. "It's time for your race to know the truth about your past and to join the fight against Dark Brother."

One of the men, a bodyguard I recognized as a well-known face at Moa's side, shook his head, backing away. "We will remain and wait for the return of our mistress."

Well, that wasn't going to happen any time soon. Instead of arguing, I whispered a request across the veil and was unsurprised when Jiao appeared almost immediately. She ignored me in favor of her people, black bob shining around her olive cheeks, dark eyes cold and uncompromising.

"Moa will not return," she said and I wondered at her harsh tone. But they seemed to expect and welcome it, focusing on the young *lóng* like they hadn't with Max. "Our time is now. And Doombringer is our new mistress."

I wasn't sure that was the right way to go, but they turned to me as one and bowed. Great, just what I needed. I'd had enough issues breaking my werefriend and the queen of the werenation, Charlotte, from her bond to me when she'd decided she owed me her life. The last thing I wanted was a bunch of evolved drach thinking I was their messiah.

"Doombringer." The leader—he must have been, looking enough like Jiao I wondered if they were related, "what will you have us do?"

Sigh. "Go with the drach," I said, pointing at Max's Stronghold portal. "And do as they tell you."

They marched without further question. I caught myself grinning as my demon spoke up.

Now, if only everyone else would just do what they're told, she grumbled.

I closed the way back to the vampire mansion, Piers and Varity joining me momentarily in Nepal then passing through to the Stronghold. There was a time when this place would have been full of Enforcers from the North American Witches Council, and another when my coven and refugees of the ill-fated Brotherhood/Witch alliance were welcome. But the betrayal of Erica Plower changed all that. When the Enforcers joined forces with the Brotherhood, the Stronghold's fury at the alliance meant the end of their habitation. If the Stronghold's soul was still present, he would have prevented Varity from passing into his plane. As it was, the theft of the heart of Creator, taken by Trill Zornov at a time I still trusted her, meant this place was no longer awake and aware. I still missed his deep, graveled voice and depth of spirit. Had to do something about getting him back, if I could.

I still felt saddened by his loss, my sneakers squeaking softly on the polished floor of the Stronghold's main foyer, glitter of the portal mirror on my far left. He might not have been much of a conversationalist, but I longed for the weight of his presence if only because that would mean the heart was in the right place.

No metaphor there or anything.

I opened my mouth to ask Max what his plans were for the *lóng* a faint smile on my face as Jiao hugged the two kids, when yet another blow hit me so hard I stumbled to my knees in shock.

SHAYLEE. Oh no, not again. And not the Sidhe, not this quickly. Everonus just mentioned it and the vampire disappearance had taken months. But as my Sidhe princess soul reached for her mother I realized what Max had been trying to tell me, something I'd lost sight of in the last few hours of lights, camera, action.

The disintegration of the Universe was speeding up.

ELEVEN

I felt the realm crumbling before I even passed over the veil line shielding it from my plane. When Aiolainn created the realm, she used the veil's own magic to turn a pocket of space into her own private playground. I had no idea how, though Cian's soul had been part of the deal, clearly. Now I'd been drach and intimately connected to the veil, it was easier to see how she'd used Cian and his spirit to form a chamber, like a tumor truth be told, bubbling off the side of my plane. Good thing the space in the veil was vast, though I wondered if the plane next to mine was affected by the press of the bubble against it. A curiosity for another time if the entire Universe didn't collapse, maybe. For now, I had the Sidhe to worry about.

Gone was the glamor of the Seelie court, the green grass and blue sky, the stunning forest and arching silver and gold bridge. Instead, blackness loomed over the trembling Sidhe, Seelie and Unseelie alike huddling as a massive cloud poised to devour them. I felt outside it and yet connected to it as Shaylee tried to reach her mother.

The queen surged to the front of the pack, arms outstretched toward us. Her perfect beauty had vanished, elongating her face, her hands, her ears until she appeared more alien than Fey, the true form of the Sidhe showing through. I shivered at the sight as Shaylee gasped and shivered when my demon took firm hold of her on one side, my vampire on the other and cut the thick, green cord of magic holding her to Aoilainn.

You mustn't, my demon growled.

We need you, my vampire sent.

Please, I whispered to the Sidhe princess as she sobbed and turned her back on her mother. *Don't leave us.*

Aoilainn wailed her loss, more complete in that moment than even when Shaylee had died so long ago. There was nothing I could do and when I met her eyes at last, when the queen of the Sidhe lowered her chin from her howl of hurt and stared at me with her glowing gaze, I felt her defeat and resignation.

Save the Universe, she sent as her people vanished in clusters and groups around her, the Unseelie going first as King Ohdran and Queen Niamh grimly waved their farewell before disappearing. *And come for us when you are successful.*

You think I'm going to succeed. It came out dull and hurtful.

Aoilainn's power snapped, faded as the black consumed her. *You always do.*

And then she was gone and the Sidhe with her.

There was no battle to keep Shaylee, not like with my vampire, though we had to scramble backward into the veil to avoid being sucked down into the void when the bubble of Aoilainn's creation popped like a giant blister. I gasped into the dimness and hugged myself while Max, oddly in human form next to me, sighed his sadness.

Sydlynn, he sent. *I fear I know why things are speeding up.*

Great. That didn't sound promising. *Do I want to know?*

He met my gaze, his diamond eyes sad. *The pieces,* he sent. *There has to be a connection.*

We're working as fast as we can to return them. Okay, snappish much, missy? But Max was shaking his head.

No, Syd, he sent, turning away from me, heading back to the Stronghold plane. *I now believe with every piece we return, we speed the destruction of the Universe.*

He *what? Wait a second.* I grasped his arm as we settled on the stone of the foyer again, the veil hiccupping closed behind us. *I thought we were supposed to put Creator back together?*

Max didn't say anything, bottomless hurt in his eyes.

Just freaking fantastic.

"With every piece we return," he said at last, "magic flees into the void."

I wanted to argue, to fight him over his reasoning. But as I thought it through, I understood. The first vampires to disappear did so right around the time Trill stole the heart of Creator from this very place. Might have been before—I strained my memory to decide which came first—might have been after. But Sebastian and Alison and the Blood Clan DeWinter's vanishing was close enough to the theft of the heart I had to admit the possibility remained Max was more than likely right.

"How long have you suspected?" I grit my teeth against his answer.

"Since the last piece's return," he said. Could have mentioned it.

"Can I ask a question?" Piers was still there, amazing. I'd lost track of him, of Varity, both watching and waiting patiently, bless them. But it seemed the Steam Union leader's patience had worn out.

I shrugged, tired suddenly, rubbed raw to the bone. "If I have an answer it will be a miracle." At least, that was how things felt. "Ask."

He nodded, accepting. "If putting Creator back together is necessary to save the Universe, but doing so is sucking all magic and magical races—"

"And planes," Varity piped up helpfully.

"And planes," he said, "then what's the bloody

point?"

"Excellent question," I said. "Thanks for asking, Mr. Obvious."

Piers grinned, shrugged. "You're welcome."

Nice to see someone wasn't freaking out. Because my heart was pounding so fast I was sure it would take off to parts unknown without me any second now.

"Another stupid question," Varity said in her gravel voice. "Just for variety." Comedians. Even in the worst of times. Which was, of course, why I loved them. "Say you succeed in finding all the missing flotsam and jetsam, what happens when Creator's statue is all nice and whole again?"

Max shuddered next to me, though he didn't respond with fear, just calm.

"I don't know," he said. "Though I have a feeling we're going to find out." When he met my eyes, my heart stopped its sudden racing. "Doombringer."

He had to say that, didn't he?

"There's nothing we can do about that right now, am I correct?" I prodded Max's power with my own, deciding then and there I'd only worry about what I could change. Screw the Universe and Creator. She'd gotten us into this mess, she could handle her own crap until I had definitive answers and actions to take. Namely, if Fate got off her scrawny ass and Zoe Helios actually landed a roadmap of Do This Now in my hands.

Max nodded.

"Okay then," I said, turning back to my friends. "Since the Universe can fall apart without us, we'll let it do its thing and we'll get back to the matter at hand." I drew a breath. "Femke."

"Jean Marc," Piers said, shaking his head, sad but grim.

"Tallah." Varity's tone matched his exactly. They sounded like bad things were about to happen to those specific people.

"Creator's arm." Max's soft finish wrapped up the whole guilt package in a nice, shiny bow.

Looked like friendship would have to wait after all. I hated to admit it, knew I should reach out and at least explain to Quaid why I was leaving him hanging instead of rushing to the rescue as I said I would. But Max's little reveal was enough to make my decision for me despite my desire to the contrary. Fate was calling again, it seemed, and I wasn't about to argue.

It was a grim group that trouped our way back through the veil and into Mom's office at Harvard. She had the right to hear what happened to the vampires and Sidhe first hand. I was shocked to see she wasn't alone, though.

"How?" I ran one hand through the silky, thick fur of the giant hound standing on her right, Galleytrot's black eyes flaring with red fire.

"Queen Aoilainn severed our Sidhe magic before the end," he said in a voice like a spring thunderstorm, sadness in him but a new determination. He'd left us a broken dog, guilt over his inability to protect Liam and Gabriel driving him to return to his master, Gwynn ap Nudd of the Wild Hunt. A blessing, from what I understood, allowing him to join the love of his heart, Mom's old second, Erica Plower. That second hound waited on Mom's left, slimmer and slightly smaller than Galleytrot, but just as grim.

"Erica," I said.

"Darae," she said in return. "My hound name, if you please, Syd."

I nodded to her. I maybe should have still held animosity toward her. After all, it was Erica who triggered all of this, wasn't it? By joining forces with Belaisle and the Brotherhood, starting off the rolling boulder of doom we'd caught barreling toward us. But I knew enough about Fate to understand she was just a tool, as much as I was. And seeing her in the form of a hound after feeling her regret and broken realization at her trial, I decided to let bygones just go the hell away and accept things were happening exactly as Fate intended.

We really had to have a talk about that at some point. So I could express my dissatisfaction with the way the game was run.

"Sydlynn Hayle, Doombringer, and company." Mom

bowed her head a moment before her shoulders squared, eyes dark and full of fire. "Under order of the North American Witches Council, I order you," *forgive the wording, sweetheart*, "to immediately retrieve Tallah Hensley and bring her to me under charge of treason against all witchdom."

I embraced her with my magic. *Forgiven*, I sent, feeling how shaken she was by the loss of her spirit power—her earth magic clinging by a thread, tied to the black hounds at her sides—by the idea that Tallah might make the same mistake as Erica. My mother's gaze lingered on the smaller hound, even as the dog now known as Darae licked the back of her hand.

"No, Mom," I said. "This one's on me. I'm taking full responsibility for what happens to Tallah and her coven. And I want you to stay out of it." *Might I suggest*, I sent in a private aside, *while I'm busy, you share with the hounds what I gave to you? Just in case.*

Mom didn't respond but from the tightening around her eyes she understood. When I stepped into the veil with Piers and Varity, the two black dogs still flanking my pale faced mother, I had faith both were willing and able to do whatever it took to make sure she had the backup she needed. No matter how this went down. Because regardless of how things ended, I was about to see to it through by whatever means necessary the Brotherhood never troubled anyone again.

TWELVE

Maybe I should have been hurt Max left me to my own business, but I knew him better than that. He departed for the Stronghold without a word and minus judgment, so I took his lack of comment on face value and did what I had to do.

I didn't bother trying to locate the Brotherhood or their leader. I didn't need to. I had a different goal in mind. If Jean Marc Dumont was in cahoots with Tallah, I wouldn't have to go looking.

Believe me, after I was done with her she'd take me right to him.

The familiar beach welcomed me, though I knew the Hensley power wasn't so kind, pushing through the barriers Tallah set up around her coven house while the Pacific Ocean washed its way against the shoreline.

I could have just opened the veil in the kitchen/living

room combo. I could have shown up without warning and grabbed Tallah, choking her like the vermin she was. Could have. Didn't. Because the perverse and furious part of me wanted her to know I was coming.

Wanted her to try to fight back. As she did, ineffectual power beating against mine. I stomped my way up the back stairs and through the glass doors, grimly pleased to see the mix of terror and rage on her dark skinned face. In her deep brown eyes. The way she trembled with tension while I stormed through her house. Through her defenses. With a snarl that had been building since I first found out what she was up to, I pinned her to the counter with a fist of magic steel.

She choked on the pressure, bending backward, clawing at her throat and the pressure there. For a heartbeat I faltered, at least inwardly. Wondered if I'd made a mistake, if the elder council had led me astray for no reason. Until sorcery crawled out of her and tried to fight back.

Yes, she could have acquired it on her own. But I had excellent reason to believe she'd had her dark power woken by the wrong kind of people.

"Syd! No!" Sashenka, my former second and Tallah's ever faithful sister, broke my need to kill the Hensley leader, but only barely. I glanced away for a heartbeat, saw the terror on her face, then ignored it, turning back to the struggles of the witch in my grasp.

Might I suggest, my vampire sent, calm and collected with a hint of sarcasm, *we keep her alive long enough to ask her questions?*

Screw that, my demon snarled. *She has nothing to tell us. Just kill her, Syd.*

Shaylee had recovered enough from her mother's disappearance she piped in. Though the sweet voice I was used to had been roughened by grief. So had her attitude, apparently. *Rip her head off and feed it to demon*, she snarled before hiking in a sob.

Nothing else would have reined me in, not Max or my mother or even Creator. But the three of them? They had more sway over me than anyone in my life and feeling Shaylee's grief was enough to cool my temper and back me up a pace.

I didn't release Tallah, but I did ease up enough she was able to draw a breath, warming the gray cast to her skin as she managed some oxygen.

"You will tell me," I said in a voice that shook while my three hitchhikers paused to listen, "where I can find Jean Marc Dumont and the Brotherhood. Or I'll kill you right now."

Tallah didn't answer, but Shenka's anger hit me like a blow I barely felt. It was only our old association that triggered the realization she was hammering at the edges of my power. "Let her go," she said, her own voice cracking. "Now, Syd." Her dark gaze flickered to her sister and back to me. "We have no idea what you're talking about." Fury shook her. Her dark skin flushed a deeper red as emotion washed through her. Outrage. Really? "How dare you barge in here and accuse my sister—"

I silenced her with a short wave of my hand before turning back to Tallah. "This is on you," I said. "I'll make sure the whole of witchdom knows it, too." She flinched before falling still while Shenka gasped. "Tell me or by the elements and Creator, Tallah, I swear I will kill you."

And I meant it. I'd only killed a few times before. The first, Ameline. The second was the Mafia leader, Nickolay Vetrov. Of course I'd also slain creatures of the other Universe, but I didn't count them because I didn't have time to get to know them, to talk to them or feel their hearts beating, hear their thoughts. Not like I thought I'd known Tallah. We'd been friends once, a lifetime or two ago, when we were both the youngest coven leaders against the rest of the North American Council. Until she blamed me for poaching her sister as my second, proceeding to steal her back again and blame everyone but herself for the attack of the Brotherhood that laid her coven low.

And now, here she was working with them, the very sorcerers who killed her family.

Bile rose in the back of my throat, but it was Shenka's soft weeping that pulled me further from the edge and made me think, listen.

"No," my former friend said, whispered while the other witches in the room—a pair of werewolves among them—stared and shook. "No, please, Tallah." Shenka gasped a breath before speaking again, one hand over her trembling lips. "Tell Syd she's wrong."

Tallah didn't say anything, renewed defiance glaring back through dark eyes.

Shenka sobbed once, stilled, before looking up at me, horror on her face. "Please," she tried again. "Please, Syd. She's my sister."

I couldn't let compassion in. Not when so much was at stake. Tallah had to believe I'd follow through. I cut Shenka off with a scowl and clamped down on her sister again, the Hensley leader crying out as my power hurt her.

Okay, it felt like crap doing it now I had possession of myself again.

Let me, my demon sent.

But no, I'd told Mom and I meant it—this was on me.

"You can't do this," Shenka's last stab at saving her sister hurt me as much as I was hurting Tallah. "The Witches Council—"

"The Council your sister abandoned and from which she emancipated this family." Piers spoke before I could, jaunty tone mocking. "That council, Shenka?"

She stared at him in mute appeal but Piers was

probably more invested in finding the Brotherhood at this point than I was. At least in his own mind.

"We're not here for the Council," I said. "I'm above the law now, didn't you know that?" A flash of anger tore through me, making my jaw ache as I ground my teeth together. "When will you people get it through your damned thick witch skulls? I'm trying to save the Universe here. The Universe." I shook Tallah with my power, knocking her against the counter as she squirmed. "I am sick," another shake, "and tired," dishes tumbled to the floor, shattering around her feet, "of this petty, pathetic crap." I dropped her to her knees in the shards, pushing her down until she was on the palms of her hands, panting for air.

With three strides I was at her side, letting my demon out, amber fire blazing around me, smoke rising from her hair while that persona whispered in Tallah's ear. "We're ready to make an example of you," she said through my lips. "And while you might think someone will swoop in and save you, that I'm too kind hearted to take your life, be assured, Tallah Hensley, if you're in bed with the Brotherhood, nothing in this Universe or the next will save you."

"Syd." Shenka, dear Shenka. Unwilling to just shut the hell up.

"You said I only had tools in my life in place of people I cared about," I said, staring into Tallah's eyes but speaking to her sister. "Turns out you traded one master for another." I jerked the leader to her feet with one hand on her arm, removing the crushing weight of my energy from her chest and throat, but trapping her with all the magic at my disposal. Her sorcery whimpered and fled beneath her in response to my white magic.

Monster after all? Check.

Tallah tried to find her defiance again, but I'd crushed it out of her. She used to be so beautiful to me, so strong and powerful, in control. The woman who clutched at her chest, who bit her lip and shot me a petulant and impotent glare seemed, instead, a waste of space and magic.

"It's true," she said, chin rising. Where she found the courage to admit it I'll never know, though I had to at least give her thin props for not trying to deny it.

If you say so, my demon growled.

Shenka's weeping resumed, though quiet and resigned as her sister spoke to her coven. More of them had gathered, the werewolves she'd adopted, her former second, gaping and astonished, witches who watched with horror as their leader owned up.

Tallah's voice entreated them as she went on. "The Brotherhood is different now." I couldn't help the snort of utter disbelief that escaped me at her blindness. Was this what Erica told herself, too, before allowing Belaisle and his people to murder one third of all North American witches? "Jean Marc is a good leader. He has a vision for their future that goes beyond Liander Belaisle and his evil ways."

Just keep telling yourself those lies, sweetie, my demon sent.

How could she be so misguided? Shaylee mentally wrung her hands, waffling between anger and sadness. *How?*

Foolishness, my vampire sent, quiet, disappointed. It wasn't until Tallah met my eyes I realized she'd heard all three of them speak, that they'd allowed it. And doubt lived in her. Even she didn't believe it herself.

Oh, Tallah.

"What have you done?" Shenka's grief turned to rage so quickly I was slow in stopping her. My shields, softened by surprise, fell enough the younger sister reached the older. Shenka carried Tallah the rest of the way to the ground, her right hand slapping across her leader's face. "After everything you said, after everything you've done. How could you betray us like this?"

That was the worst of it, wasn't it? The fact Tallah's judgment of Erica and the Council led here, to the exact same mistakes made all over again.

"It's not the same thing," Tallah whispered to her sister, looking dazed and lost as Shenka's hand hovered, ready to strike again. I'd never seen the younger Hensley so angry, or even seen her raise her hand to anyone, anything. "He's helping make us stronger." Tallah's sorcery showed up, cowed and reaching for her sister, but

Shenka slapped it away with her own, though the need to hit her leader seemed to have left her.

I pulled back, my own anger dying, just weary at the sight of the two sisters hating each other and wondering where we'd all gone so very wrong.

"You don't understand, Shenka." Tallah grasped at her while my old second stood, pulling away with abject disgust on her face. "Something huge is coming." Her gaze flickered to me, back to her sister. That was an understatement. "I've seen the piece of Creator Jean Marc holds. It's shown me what's coming and we need to be ready."

All the information I needed, thanks. I grasped Tallah firmly again, drew her to her feet with magic while her sister turned her back. "Awesome," I said, fake cheer matching the tight grin on Piers's face. "Let's go see it together, shall we?"

I handed her off to Varity who clasped the Hensley leader's wrists in blue fire.

"While you're outside the law," the old Enforcer said with a hint of amusement, "I have a Council leader to answer to."

"When I'm done with her," I said. "Tallah. Where is he?"

She shuddered, looked away. My jaw hurt a lot. Too much clenching in just a short period of time. I'd send her the bill for my dentist.

"Allow me." Piers stepped up before I could protest or interfere and pressed his fingertips to her forehead. She screamed immediately, but her pain didn't stop me from following him into her mind and taking what we needed.

Yes, I was uncomfortable with what we were doing. This kind of rape was exactly that and I had my limits, didn't I? Or did I? Damn it.

Just damn it.

The first image made me want to throw up. The way she thought of him, his body against hers... lovers. She was sleeping with Jean Marc Dumont. I almost left her mind then and there, to throw up everything I'd ever eaten or wipe my brain on a piece of sandpaper or just find a way to erase the disgusting images from my poor, abused memory. But Piers was still going and I followed the bull on the leash deeper into dark territory.

I know this place, he sent to me, the sight of fire and stone walls and some kind of chapel making him pause. *Bollocks, why didn't I think of it?*

Where? I retreated from her mind, Piers with me, finding the Hensley leader sagging in Varity's grasp, blood running from her nose. The pressure of our search had knocked her out.

Zoe's old home, Piers sent, grim and angry. *The Sanctuary.*

THIRTEEN

"That's enough." The diminutive werewoman's voice drew me around, Nina Dillon's face dark and grim. The former member of Cicero Caine's werepack bowed her head to me, head shaved showing faint scars in the dark stubble, tattooed arms straight at her sides, piercings catching the light through the glass doors. "We had no idea, you must believe that. But we can't stand by and let you kill our leader."

That had better not be a challenge, my demon snarled.

Whatever. I shrugged and turned away even as Nina spun on Shenka. "You must step up," she said while the younger Hensley wiped at the last of the tears on her face. "We need a new leader and you're of the bloodline."

Shenka gaped at her but my vampire sighed.

It's time, Syd, she sent. *We both know what has to happen here.*

We could let Shenka take over, I sent, heart hurting at last. This was a disaster, really. The end of a formerly powerful family. I knew what she was thinking, what my other personas were thinking. But we were down so many covens after the Brotherhood attacks. Could we afford to disband one?

We can't trust her not to try to avenge her sister. I'm sorry. For my vampire to say it, she had to be right. I knew she was, understood before I even left Harvard what the end result of this visit to California would mean.

The end of the Hensley family once and for all.

Mom must have known, too. And when I connected with her, she didn't seem surprised to hear from me.

Just be gentle, she sent. *This isn't the Dumont coven you're disbanding.* I didn't bother mentioning I had nothing to do with the loss of that particular witchline. Charlotte's curse on Andre and his own cruel decision to deny Jean Marc the family magic led to their end. Still, I'd been witness to it, so I knew what Mom meant. *The Hensley's have been, until now, a faithful and proactive family.* She sighed in my head, so tired. I knew the feeling. *I don't have the right to interfere. But once the witches are free of the Hensley magic, they are welcome to join other covens in this territory.*

Good enough for me.

Even as Shenka hovered, undecided, staring at her sister, I stepped in and grasped the Hensley family magic in my power and pulled it free from Tallah by the root. It struggled in my grasp, though not that hard. It must have understood how far its leader had fallen. And though I was still tempted to hand it off, could see the fear in Shenka's eyes, the resignation falling over her face, I simply couldn't risk it. Not now.

Instead, I shattered the family power into enough pieces it split equally among all the registered members of the old coven, driving the shards into the individual witches and werewolves. They gasped as a group, their voices carrying from the distance where those of the family listened and watched in absentia. With a push of energy, I severed their link to one another and burned the connections permanently as I spoke to each and every one of them.

"Hear me," I said. "The Hensley coven is no more." Shenka's lower lip trembled though anger woke in her eyes. "Never again will you be able to link to each other or form family magic in that name." I'd never done this before, knew there was precedent but felt the pressure of the magnitude of what I was creating as I went on. "The North American Witches Council has made it clear to me you will be welcome, as individuals, to join covens in that territory. But from henceforth, no former Hensley witch will be able or permitted to combine with another."

And that was that. Far easier, I think, than such a task should have been. I turned my back on Shenka, knowing she would hate me from now on, where once she just held me in contempt. Fine, let her. She'd made her bed, chosen her family. And it wasn't mine.

She was dead to me from now on.

I spun and glared at Tallah who had regained consciousness in time to realize what I'd done. She screamed out loud, a blood curdling sound echoing through the silent house, seeking the family power that had once been hers, meeting only silence.

"Jean Marc!"

Any sympathy I might have felt died at that cry. And Shenka thought *I* was a monster. Her own sister had sold her out to the Brotherhood. If she was going to hate anyone, Tallah should have been her first choice.

"How dare you?" Shenka's voice shuddered, stilled.

Varity answered for me. "Be grateful," the old Enforcer said, "that Miriam and the Council don't sweep in here and burn the lot of you at the stake. You're off easy, girlie. Now, get lost."

I could hear Shenka crying again, didn't care. Hardened my heart to it as I nodded to Piers.

"You have the location?" Of course he did. I just needed something official to say, a distraction.

"Right here." He tapped his forehead, smart enough not to vocalize the sympathy on his face. Must have helped he thrummed with excitement. Could hardly blame him. This little side trip had little to do with his ultimate goal.

Frankly, I was tired of being waylaid. Time to put an end to Jean Marc and the Brotherhood. Permanently.

And yet, I couldn't help but flinch as we left in the black tunnel of Piers's power when Shenka's magic, weak and charred at the edges, slammed into my back.

I'll be seeing you, Syd, she sent.

My demon snarled in return, cutting her off. *Looking forward to it.*

Shenka retreated as the tunnel closed behind us.

FOURTEEN

The stone corridor on the other side of Piers's tunnel felt mundane and comfortable, almost like the Stronghold, except this place was darker, without windows and I could tell without scanning we were deep underground.

Beneath Los Angeles, Piers sent, tight and focused. *This way*.

So he'd been here before, enough he knew where to go? Excellent. Saved us from hunting through what was feeling like a bit of a maze to me already.

It felt odd, just the two of us. And yet, we'd been here many times before, hadn't we? My heart lightened just a bit at the memory of the pair of us storming the werewolf palace in Ukraine so long ago. How young I'd been, how full of myself. I was able to see that now, to understand just how much of a mess I'd managed to make barreling my way through the world in search of my werefriend. Charlotte's rescue came at the destruction of the Black Souls—and nearly the werepalace—and was my first encounter with Eva Southway and the rest of the Steam Union.

While I knew there was little time for reminiscence, somehow walking down this stone corridor with flame flickering from small cul-de-sacs, torches that burned but released no smoke lighting the way far better than ordinary fire, drew me down memory lane. Maybe it was reconnecting with Piers, or the fact I needed something to anchor to as we entered the unknown yet again. Whatever the reason, in that moment I was grateful with a surge of emotion so powerful it shook me that Piers was at my side.

He jerked to a halt, turned to meet my eyes, his own grays wide and full of regret. "Syd," he choked. Hesitated.

I just nodded, swallowed my guilt and grief at our conflict. "I know," I said. "I'm sorry. More than you'll ever understand."

Piers hugged me then, hard and swift, and I crushed him to me with the same fervor he used. So silly, really, to stand there in enemy territory embracing my friend when we should have been focused on the task at hand. Any moment we could be set upon by bad guys. But this felt important, more so than anything in the Universe right now.

Piers finally let me go, wiping at his cheeks with one hand, a faint smile on his wide mouth. Gone was the pull that aged him, smoothed out were the lines on his brow. He still had the deep, dark circles under his eyes, was far too lean for my liking, but the transformation was complete. My friend had come back to me.

Awesome.

The lightness I felt at our reconciliation made me giddy. Grinning like an idiot, I grasped his hand in mine and swung our arms like we were kids.

"Well, Steam Union," I said. "Shall we go kick some Brotherhood ass?"

"After you." He swept a bow toward me but kept his grip on my hand.

And that was how, moments later, beaming smiles that should have been scowls, we strode with glee through the wide, wooden doors and into the chapel in Sanctuary and came face to face with Jean Marc Dumont.

Correction. Jean Marc Dumont and about fifty Brotherhood sorcerers.

I laughed out loud. Nothing could shatter my mood. And seeing his frown, the way he twitched nervously at the end of the aisle between the rows of benches, his short, dark hair heavy over his lowered brow, just made me happier.

"Hey," I waved with my free hand.

Jean Marc gaped at me, at Piers, before shaking his

head and gathering his power. A wall of black formed between us and him, between me and my goal as I spotted, just past his right shoulder, the arm of Creator resting on the altar of the chapel.

"Perfect," I said, striding forward, while shattering and dispersing the collective shield of the gathered Brotherhood. "I've been looking for that."

I hurt them, oh, my, yes. Even as I created some significant property damage in the ancient looking chapel. Wooden benches shattered with sharp explosions blocked from harming me with shielding, old, worn stone cracking and blowing apart, striking sparks where the shards landed. A shame to cause such havoc in this revered place where once Zoe's people had clearly worshipped. But then again, the focus of their worship had been a dying maji, Gaia, her magic slowly siphoned over time by the disgusting Liander Belaisle. So I found it hard to really give a crap if I pulled the place down or not.

I heard their cries of agony, knew Piers flexed his own magic muscles when his white power joined with mine, swirling into the blackness of the Brotherhood's energy. It fractured over and over as they tried to muster defense and, as the last of them collapsed, drained and in deep seated hurt, I laughed again, this time only feet from where Jean Marc glared, body shaking with rage.

"So predictable," I said, coming to a firm halt before him with Piers strong and tall at my side. "Had you shared, you would have beaten us or at least escaped." I flickered my fingers at him, white sorcery stirring against his. "But I knew you better than that, Jean Marc. No way would you ever give up the power you'd stolen." He flinched, glanced at Piers with a flare of fear, then back to me with his dull, accusing eyes. "I'm so looking forward to this."

"Syd." The sound of his voice made me stop, turned me slightly around. I caught sight of Demetrius in the periphery, the now hundred or so sorcerers who had us surrounded, more filing in by the moment. There was enough grief in his voice I knew my Demetrius still lived inside him. But his power belonged to the Brotherhood.

Jean Marc's smirk told me he had no idea he'd lost. This little show of power? How pathetic.

"You must think Syd incapable of harming those she cares about to get what she wants." Piers's tone came out light, carefree as he tossed his long, blond hair over his shoulder. "And maybe that's the case. But don't ever underestimate me, Jean Marc." In a flash, my friend's expression flattened, darkened. And the screaming began.

I let Piers handle the Brotherhood, like I had a choice in the matter. I had the angry Dumont before me to deal with. Not to mention the fact the Steam Union leader had about a lifetime of hurt to pay back in kind. And though Jean Marc hadn't shared his newfound white sorcery, though those of his kind were easy to deal with thanks to it, he had the power I did.

But I didn't care how the battle turned out, not really. Not when there was something more important than the death of Jean Marc to think about. *Gabriel.* I sent the message as tightly as possible. *Get Max. And come. I have the arm.*

My son's affirmation was all the word I needed. He'd handle his side of it, with the help of the drach leader. Leaving me, at last, to finally end the Dumont family's evil once and for all.

Jean Marc's power leached through the stones at my feet, trying to trap me, but I'd been here before. Funny how old memories jogged during times like this. His face could have been Ameline's, his mocking grin her tight, dark smile of success. Except when the white sorcery he controlled rose to grasp me in its grip, it met mine, full on.

"Old news, I'm afraid," I said as I gestured, a javelin of gleaming white leaping for his chest. He blocked it with a curse, slamming me with a fist of his own. "That's your problem, Jean Marc," I said, dancing aside with agility I didn't realize I had, slicing forward at calf level with a thin blade of magic. It took him at the calf, cutting a wedge out of his shielding and sending him to one knee. Roaring his fury, he battered at me with two hammers of white power that did nothing against my shields. "No finesse."

My son appeared through a Gateway behind the Brotherhood leader, practically landing on top of the altar. Sassafras and Jiao flashed through behind him, no sign of Max. For whatever reason, at least Gabriel had backup.

Nice work, Mom! My son's excitement made me grin and wave at him while Jean Marc spun, animal fury trying to reach Gabriel. He might as well have lay down at my feet and offered his throat.

Everything went away when Jean Marc's power focused on my kid. Everything. Except the uncontrollable need to kill.

I staggered forward with my power wrapping around Jean Marc's thick neck. It was only when something hit me hard between the shoulder blades I realized this wasn't over yet. Not by a long shot.

Not when Liander Belaisle and Eva Southway stormed past me, floating on a platform of sorcery, hurtling toward my son and the arm of Creator.

Why did everything freeze in that moment? Why did indecision—painful and wrenching—jerk me to a halt at the sight? Kill Jean Marc. Stop Belaisle. Kill Jean Marc. Stop Belaisle. Like a massive war sprang up inside me, I felt the two powerful needs run headlong into each other and pin me in place as the world spun on around me.

Never before had I felt such contention, the girls locked into it as tightly as myself. And even as events wound out before me, milliseconds really, barely heartbeats, I felt like the statue we were trying to recreate.

Belaisle turned his head in the slow motion my life had become, smiling at me, darkness in his yellow eyes. And lunged for the piece of Creator while my son leaped in his way.

No. No, please. Save Gabriel. *Not my son!*

And then, in a flare of white, she appeared. Trill Zornov stood between the form of Belaisle, still falling, and my son, now draped over the piece. Belaisle hit her like he'd rammed an immovable wall and bounced back with a shout of surprise and pain.

Jean Marc froze in place, panting, but I could finally move. The shock of Trill's arrival had shattered the war inside me and allowed me to drive a fist of white sorcery into the Brotherhood leader's back, carrying him to the floor where I pinned him in a net of the same magic. His own fluttered against me, but I piled on more power as I gaped at Trill and tried to figure out just what the hell was actually happening.

"Out of the way, girl." Eva's voice sounded about as welcoming as a buzz saw in full blare. Piers wavered beside me but I held out one hand, holding him back. I had lost all trust in Trill when she'd stolen the heart of Creator and betrayed me over and over again. This was the first time I saw any indication she hadn't lied to me when she said she was on my side.

I needed to know what was going on.

"Not this time." Trill's voice carried, calm and quiet. Her slim body stood firm, her power holding off the former Steam Union leader and, when he recovered enough to rise, Belaisle who joined Eva in pushing against the young woman who had been my friend.

I felt their power, the edges of it. Let them shove and batter and jerk on the barrier she'd created between herself and the altar. And did nothing to help her. Because I needed to know, damn it.

It might sound like this took long moments, that I had all the time in the world to absorb what was happening. Truthfully? Maybe fifteen seconds. Enough for Piers to turn to me and glare, to reach for his mother again. And for Eva to pull free of her fight against Trill and grasp Belaisle's hand, a dark tunnel forming beside her.

They were running. No. Freaking. Way.

Let them go. Trill's voice in my head, reassuring, so very relaxed. *It's not yet time, Syd. Just let them run.*

I did, holding Piers back, trusting for the first time maybe, just maybe, Trill wasn't my enemy after all. Wondering even as the evil pair fled—Belaisle snarling his fury at me—just who Trill was working for.

There is an order to everything, Trill sent. *And to everything an order.*

That sounds familiar, I sent, harsher than I intended as

the Brotherhood collectively collapsed and Jean Marc's howl of defeat rang in the small chapel. *You and Zoe are tight these days. Mind telling me just what that means?*

Trill looked up, met my eyes, a soft, kind smile on her face though her dark eyes brimmed with sadness. *I miss you*, she whispered in my head. She paused another moment, then nodded, looking down. *Pay attention when Wilding Springs goes dark.* Another pause. *Listen to your heart.* She sounded like she'd said more than she intended. And, with that, she vanished.

More questions than answers. How original.

FIFTEEN

Piers spun me around and hugged me, despite the fact doing so could have jarred loose my control of Jean Marc. Who was I kidding? It was only then I realized my friend had layered his own white sorcery on top of the tight and painful cage I'd build around the prone form of the Brotherhood leader. And that the room was getting very, very crowded, the youthful, furious faces of the Steam Union appearing in tunnels of darkness as he called in his cavalry to contain their enemies.

"Syd." He swung me side to side before setting me down, a bit breathless, eyes shining. "You know what this means?"

I did. "The end to the Brotherhood." I grinned at him, suddenly elated myself. How long had we been working toward this? And I'd only been part of the fight for a decade or so. Piers and his people had been fighting for centuries.

It had to feel good.

"Gabriel." Piers turned his attention to my son who no longer hunched over the arm, his hazel eyes quiet, little face grim. "Can you reverse it?"

Of course. The damaged Jean Marc had done, using the piece to steal Steam Union members for the Brotherhood. I opened my mouth to encourage my son to do so when Gabriel sighed and I knew things weren't going to go the way Piers wanted them to.

"I'm so sorry," he said in a voice that sounded more like Liam every day. "That's not how Creator's body is meant to be used." Piers gaped at him while Gabriel turned his attention to me, grief growing. "Mom, I need to get this to the statue before more harm can come of it."

The renewal of our friendship might be over before I had a chance to enjoy it. Piers's face darkened, that now recognizable fury rising in him. Hands clenched into fists at his sides, he gestured at the fallen Brotherhood, some of whom I knew were Steam Union converts, feeling Demetrius behind me, seeing him stagger to his feet. "Please tell me," the young Brit snarled, "you have an excellent reason to leave this mess behind when you have the power to do something about it. Because there has to be a reason." He shuddered, emotions tearing through him fast and furious. I reached for him with power but he shoved me away, left me to guard Jean Marc alone as Piers stepped back, magic building.

Aimed at my son.

Oh, *hell* no.

"Please, Piers," Gabriel said, tears tracking down his little cheeks, one hand reaching out, imploring the furious Steam Union leader. "You have to trust me. This is important." He bowed his head, shoulders sagging forward. "It's so heavy."

I knew he didn't mean to say that out loud, that my son wasn't talking to us, or about the piece. In fact, in that instant, I knew what no one else in the room could possibly know, what Gabriel really meant.

Let me carry it for you, I sent.

You have your own burden to bear. My son's head came up and he managed a small smile, one hand settling on the arm. *I'll be okay, Mom. You worried about me, when Belaisle came.* A faint hint of amusement woke in his mental touch. *You should know he can't hurt me.*

Good to know. Like that would stop me from worrying in the future.

Gabriel's good humor faded into pain again. *It'll work out,* he sent. *I promise. I just wasn't ready for how angry Piers would be.*

You can't help? I shouldn't have asked, but damn it. Piers deserved our aid if we could give it. And Demetrius… Gram would never forgive me.

Gabriel's brow furrowed as he turned, the piece in his hands, giant arm of Creator that should have been too heavy for him to carry floating along at his side. *I thought you, of all people, would know better than to ask.*

Consider me chastised. By my eight-year-old. Awesome.

Piers tried to stop him, threw a net of white sorcery at my son. But I blocked him, of course I did, while Sassafras and Jiao formed a wall of protection on the other side. I watched them go, knowing I had to follow, but took a moment to hold Piers tight, while Jean Marc began to struggle. Dividing my attention wasn't the smartest thing to do, but Piers had to understand.

He had to listen.

Let me go. His voice growled in my head. *It can't end like this, Syd. The Brotherhood has won if we are left in this mess.*

No, I sent. *Trust Gabriel.* Piers glared at me, chest heaving as he fought me. He had more than enough magic to create a bigger challenge than I had reserves for at the moment. But it was as if he just wanted me to feel his resistance. *And, if you can't trust him, Piers, trust me.*

That got him. He sagged, turned away. And lashed out with all that gathered magic at the prone figure lying before us. Jean Marc cried out in agony, blood spurting from his nose and running out of his right ear.

While I was all for killing the asshat, torture was a bit beyond my needs at the moment. Still, after saying no, who was I to deny the Steam Union leader his revenge?

We all know what vengeance leads to, my vampire sent, soft and kind. And, when Piers flinched and glanced sideways at me, guilt on his face, I knew she'd let him hear her.

"You're taking away all my fun," he said, though his tone had softened some, his body no longer rigid with fury.

"Syd." Demetrius joined us, his pale eyes meeting mine with something akin to shame though this was far from his fault. Still, after years spent insane thanks to the mercies of the Brotherhood, being one of them must have felt like the ultimate betrayal. "Just go. We'll deal with this." He gestured at Jean Marc, now unconscious on the stone. "It's our task to bear."

Piers bowed his head to the old sorcerer. "What are we going to do?" Such wistful courage in his voice. I wanted to hug him but Demetrius moved past me, gripping his former leader's arm in his hand.

"Whatever we can to make this right."

Okay then.

I left them there to deal with Jean Marc, to work out their differences. Maybe this wasn't the end we'd hoped for—a bit anti-climactic for my tastes, since I loved happy endings—but there might be a way. With the right leader, the Brotherhood at least could be less a worry and more an ally on our plane.

So why, if things were looking a bit up, did I feel like I was betraying them when I stepped through the veil and left them behind?

For the first time I realized the ribbon around my wrist felt tight and stiff, as if it were upset with something. Well, the feeling was mutual. But I had other things to worry about, bigger things. Shifting from personal and plane-wide issues to Universal ones was wearing on me, sure was.

Gabriel stood immobile before me when I appeared in the Stronghold's inner sanctum, the arm in his grasp, staring up at Max. Mabel and a handful of drach waited quietly behind their leader. While I didn't feel a wave of animosity or anger, there was clearly enough tension in the air to indicate I'd walked into a standoff.

Sass. I sent his name, tight and worried. *Tell me everything's okay?*

Depends on your definition of "okay", he sent back.

Smartass cat.

"Max." I stopped next to my son, doing my best not to sigh and shake him when he nodded to me with that same quiet, calm expression he always wore. "What's up?"

"We're waiting for you," he said.

My son glanced up at me, sadness in his face. "Max wants me to hold off on replacing the arm."

It was clear from Gabriel's tight mouth and stiff

shoulders he disagreed with the drach leader's suggestion.

Why did I suddenly feel like a TV court judge?

"Max?" I drew his name out, my frustration bubbling. "Reasoning?"

"Only that I fear my suppositions about the pieces are true," he said. "And that if Gabriel returns the arm to Creator now, we will do more harm than good."

It was the first time he didn't seem all that happy about the piece being returned. And I knew why. If Max was right, putting this piece back meant we were speeding the disintegration of the Universe.

"Maybe we should stockpile the pieces from now on." It did seem a reasonable suggestion. Until my son sighed and shook his head.

"You don't understand." So much anger in him suddenly, frustration and irritation, unlike my son. When he looked up, something else lived in his eyes. Not his father, not the boy I loved. Something I didn't recognize. But I knew the voice when I heard it.

"Creator." I gasped the name. But no. Not Creator.

The veil. The Universe itself.

Oh. My. Swearword.

Gabriel didn't acknowledge that I'd spoken. "None of you see the big picture." He lowered his head, a bull ready to charge. "I have to return the piece. Now." He took a single firm step forward. "Get out of my way, Max."

Terror gripped me, for my son and for the Universe.

What did this mean? He was becoming the veil? But no, surely not. I could keep telling myself that, make myself feel better, even as the giant, hulking form of the lord of the drach blanched when he looked in my son's eyes.

And stepped aside.

The drach hummed softly to themselves, Sassafras's hands on one side, Jiao's on the other, holding me back as my son carried the arm of Creator to the statue. I could only watch, wanting to weep, unable to help him or do anything as his small body climbed into Creator's lap and placed the arm in its former position.

The band of black at my wrist flinched a heartbeat before light flared, magic sealing the arm to the statue. I drew a breath at the pain just as the entire world heaved beneath me.

SIXTEEN

I barely felt the Stronghold shaking under my feet, not when the veil itself shrieked its agony. My magic tore at the edges and I was diving through, Max and the drach with me, Sass at my side. I gaped in horror, holding still with one hand clutching my chest as if I could keep the Universe safe even as, in a ripple of blips in the distance, entire planes snapped like rubber bands and vanished into the darkness.

How long it went on, how many we lost, I can't say. I only know I was gasping for breath into lungs that finally demanded air when the last one popped, a bubble bursting into the void. I leaned against Sass despite not needing such support inside the veil itself, the feel of his lean form necessary. Touch kept me grounded.

It was a somber group who turned and reentered the Stronghold underchamber. Gabriel sat on Creator's lap, silent and staring, while I struggled to find something to say.

"At least," Max finally said in his deep, musical voice, "we have confirmation my fears were correct."

He could say that again.

I wanted to approach Gabriel, to talk to him, but something held me back. He seemed lost within himself, struggling with who knew what. Did he feel guilt for what he'd been forced to do? I should have gone to him, been his mother. But all I could think about was what I'd seen in his eyes and the fact that I was Doombringer.

The distraction I thought I wanted—careful what you wish for, Syd—appeared through a gap in the veil as Meira strode through, her towering demon form rippling with anger and fear.

"Syd." She shuddered inside her shining cat suit, long hair swinging around her as she spun and took in the scene before speaking. Good for her for having the presence of mind to try to sort out what was up before diving into her own stuff. Which she did. "You wanted to know if demons were disappearing."

I nodded, mute, afraid.

She nodded back, grim, equally afraid. "And taking chunks of planes with them."

"The Node?" That was all we needed, for the teardrop of power holding the demonic planes together to fall apart again.

Meira shrugged, more out of frustration and lack of knowledge from what she said next. "It's fine," she growled, like that was an offense in her eyes. "Stable, strong, happy." She tossed her hands in the air, scowl so deep it darkened the red around her eyes to black. "It should be a freaking mess and it's burbling at me like it's never been so content. Even Ahbi's acting like nothing's wrong."

Weird. Our demon grandmother, her soul now embedded forever in the Node, didn't take such things lightly, never had. She was too invested—literally, now—in the wellbeing of Demonicon to take this in stride. Which meant the disintegration wasn't harming her, for now. I'd take that slice of good news. Until it turned into bad news.

Pessimist.

"It doesn't feel like last time," Meira said, beginning to pace, my favorite. "But it does, in a way. And it's got me thinking." She stopped and pinned Max with her amber eyes. "What about creating a Universal Node? Something to hold the entire veil together?"

Brilliant. Why didn't I think of that? What an excellent id—

Nope. Max's big head shook from side to side, a sigh escaping him. I hated when he sighed. It meant a big *no way, Jose* was coming.

"I wouldn't even know where to begin," he said. "The

planes of Demonicon are numbered and it is the group consciousness of the demons who live there that make binding them possible." I didn't know that, but it made sense. "How do we convince countless world inhabitants that they need to work together when they have no idea the veil and the Universe is even in danger?" Okay, he had a point. "We have only two options," he said. "Continue reassembling Creator and be the cause of the end of everything, or stop."

"From what I can tell," Meira said, "the second isn't going to make things any better."

Agreed. "And the first is supposedly what we're meant to do." Doombringer raised her ugly head. "Right?"

Max shrugged. I hated his shrug about as much as his sigh.

"You know," my sister said, all the intensity draining from her as she sagged a bit, Ruler turning into my gorgeous younger sibling for a moment, "when the time came, when I realized the end was near, giving up the bond of the Node was the only thing I could do. So I could build it again from scratch."

The fact she was suggesting we do the same thing in so many words with the vastness of the Universe made my head hurt. And yet.

And yet.

"Creator must have a plan." Max's tone had changed,

his calm returned. I wished I had his faith in Her. "She is calling the magicks home for reasons only She knows." And maybe my son. "This must be the path we need to take."

That was an about face. "So we let the Universe fall apart." Yeah, great idea. "You do realize that choice might lead to Dark Brother breaking through?"

"If that's the case," Max said with his irritating calm, "then that is Her will."

Damn it.

"This is a far cry from letting a bunch of planes revert to their natural state." Why was I the only one angry about this? No, not the only one. The black ribbon flexed on my wrist.

"You forget the Order soldiers are falling into the void as well," Mabel said. My ancestress had chosen to side with her leader, then. Fair enough. "The likelihood planes of the Dark Universe are being drawn into the void is high."

But not confirmed. Still, her logic was solid. And sent a massive shiver down my spine.

"So what you're saying is we're all going to end up in the same place." The void. "When Creator's statue is complete, we'll be stuck there, every single one of us. Including Dark Brother and the Order."

No one said anything for a long time.

"Are we done?" I spun sideways, shocked to find my

son standing just outside our group, watching us. His face had returned to himself, but whatever had lived in him remained at the edges.

I nodded, unable to think of a thing to say.

"We need to move quickly from now on." Like we hadn't been trying. Or had we? As I thought about it, I realized how much time we seemed to have wasted, months on my part. I'd felt a need to move before, but this urgency that gripped me was new.

And contrived. So, the Universe was finally ready to act, was it? Awesome.

"You have a location for another piece?" He'd stood in my son's way just a little while ago. Now, Max seemed like a complete convert to Gabriel's need.

"I don't just yet." My son's frown was his own, his frustration showing. "But I will shortly. The time is coming, though. If we don't act, if we don't replace the pieces in the precise sequence intended from this moment on, the way between will be breeched and the Order will come through." Not maybe. Not could.

Will.

Well, all righty then.

SEVENTEEN

But it was Gabriel's next statement that really did me in.

"There," he said, that single word drawing me into his magic as he showed me with a simple gesture exactly where the Universes intersected. I felt myself drawn physically to it even as my son went on. "Your guess the other Universe is disappearing is accurate, Mabel." Well, at least it wasn't just us. I examined the spot in the veil though my body remained in the Stronghold chamber. Disconcerting at first until I allowed my white sorcery to graze the edges and everything became clear.

How had I missed this scar in the fabric of the veil? It ran through every single portion of it, tendrils tying the Universe together not only with power but with a frozen moment, an instant of time that felt like a scream waiting to be released. I shuddered from it even as I was drawn to it.

It felt like doom.

"Is this my fault?" I had to ask, didn't know why it seemed so important.

"Yes," my son said, clear and without emotion. "And no." His magic hugged mine, my sweets still in there, at least.

"Have I been Doombringer all along?" Of course I had. He didn't have to answer that.

When I retreated to the Stronghold chamber, I realized two things. One, my son was my son again, the veil releasing him completely, at least for now. And two, no one else in the room had seen what I'd seen.

That weight was mine to bear. Mine and Gabriel's.

There wasn't much else we could do at that point. In our quick exodus after the shaking of the Stronghold, I'd missed who the guardian of the arm had been, the departure of his or her spirit. A shame, one I carried with guilt. Each of Max's people deserved to be honored. I left him and the drach to do just that, taking my son with me when I departed for home, Sass and Jiao joining us. But instead of returning to Wilding Springs or Harvard or any number of other places I could have gone, my heart demanded I find something good I could do in the midst of the horrible I'd just discovered.

I was the end of everything. And my son was, too.

When I stepped out onto the stone floor of the elder

council chamber below the pyramids at Giza, I wasn't in the mood for arguments. Discussions. Talking, even. And, from the looks on the faces of those who remained they understood at least in part just how I was feeling.

"Femke Svennson," I said, voice dull and tired. So tired. "I'm going to fix her now."

That was the only warning they were going to get and could consider themselves lucky I took the time to tell them. Because telling was my new way of being.

Yup.

Before I could leave, though, Everonus spoke up. "You should know," he said, "it's not us who have held her down."

That was news. Okay, I'd listen a minute before going and saving my friend. If only to get what I needed to make it happen. "Talk."

"My magic has been holding her together, truth be told." That was definitely news. The tall, handsome Sidhe looked drawn, and I realized then the very fact he was here, and not in the void with the rest of his people, was a miracle. He seemed stretched thin to me, as though his strength was failing. And I realized then it was only the magic of the elder council keeping him here on this plane, in the Universe, out of the void. I wondered how long they would be willing to sacrifice their own strength to protect him. To protect the final threads of earth magic remaining.

Not much longer, most likely.

"Something controls her," he said, beautiful voice cracking softly. "Something I have been unable to free her from or identify clearly. And, as my strength fades it takes over more and more control of her." He coughed delicately into one hand, a hand that shook from strain. "My time is short. I'm sure you are aware of the loss of the realm."

Duh. But I nodded instead of speaking that insult.

"We release you from your promise," Everonus said. "Save Femke and do what you can to restore her to power before this is over."

He knew, did he? Where this was all heading. I turned my back on him and took us home, to the place where my heart remained, to the one spot where maybe I could curl up in bed, hug the pillow that still smelled of Liam thanks to the magic of that place and try to pull myself together.

Ran into a wall of nothing before stumbling, shocked, into the basement of city hall in Wilding Springs. I spun toward the entry that should have been there, reached for it, found only stone and emptiness. And did my best not to cry while my son did it for me, holding tight to my hand as he, too, realized the truth.

The Gate. The cavern.

Gone.

It was only then, standing in the semi-dark of the

mundane basement I realized without Cian, without Aiolainn, I'd lost my chance to find Liam. So random, that thought, so outside what I should have been worrying about. And yet, if anything could make me finally break down and cry, it was knowing my darling oak tree was lost to me forever at last.

I fell to my knees next to my son, clutched his weeping form to my chest and sobbed like Liam had died all over again.

It was the touch of a known mind that drew me out of my grief. I sagged against my son as Nona reached out and gently interrupted.

She made no mention of my obvious state. Instead, she sent quietly, *Everonus is no longer with us.*

I stared blindly at the place where the cavern entrance should have been and nodded into the air as if she could see me. Noted the complete loss, now, of all earth magic outside of Shaylee, shivering and crying inside me. It wasn't right, how that giant power sighed out its ending into the void. No earthquake met its departure, no rumble of a thunderstorm in the distance to mark its passing. Just the sigh of a sad and lonely magic leaving us behind.

Understood. It took a great deal of effort to stand, to draw my son upright. Sassafras helped, his own face wet with tears, Jiao's jaw jumping as if she fought off the inevitable. Nice of them to let me grieve, though.

I needed that.

I suppose, I sent to the old maji woman, *you're as ancient as the rest of them.* Because that would just be the icing on the cake for me right now. To have been fooled into thinking she was really the Zornov's grandmother.

But her wry laughter told me otherwise. *Heaven forbid*, she sent. *I'm just a weary old woman, Syd. From a long line of maji blood who have carried this weight through the centuries. I never told you, but the Hayle family is no stranger to me. My great grandmother aided your ancestor, Auburdeen, when she needed it most.*

I had no idea.

Ask Sassafras about it, she sent. *Or, better yet, I'll tell you the story myself one day.* She paused, sad and pensive. *When this is over.*

If there was a when to look forward to.

And no, she sent. *The children have no idea I'm on the elder council, so don't give them trouble for my duplicity.*

Since Apollo and Owen already confirmed as much, I let it go.

I have to confess, she sent. *I've been training Trill to take my place, however. Something that won't happen now.*

Because the elder council will be gone with the rest of the Universe, I sent, *or because she has another destiny?* I couldn't bring myself to be angry with the younger Zornov anymore. She'd helped us, hadn't she? If only I knew what game she was playing.

Perhaps both. I loved cryptic. Not. *I feel your fear, Sydlynn*

Hayle. Yeah, it was there, creeping beneath the surface of my guilt and sorrow. No one ever accused me of a good poker face. The opposite, frankly. *And while it may not help, please know I trust in you. In what you must do and how you will succeed, no matter your worries.* At least one of us did. *And I trust Trillia.* Something that was finally growing on me, too. I felt myself relax as Nona went on. *She has a big job ahead of her. So stop being so mean to her and pay attention.*

Did she just chastise me, really?

Well, considering Trill was the reason we had the arm back in place, I was willing to finally consider maybe the Zornov maji had an important role to play in this, too. I just wished things could be easy for once, straight forward.

As if.

Nona let me go while I looked down into my son's sad face.

"I'm sorry," he choked. "It's all gone because I had to put the piece back."

No way was he carrying this alone. Forget trying to relieve him of his burden completely. I knew better from intimate experience. But at least he could have some help lugging the baggage around.

"You're a Hayle as much as an O'Dane," I said, brushing reddish blond curls back from his cheeks. "Tough choices are our way of life, sweets. I wish it could be otherwise. But I'm here, we're all here." I felt Sass's magic answer kindly, the shift in his power as he took cat form. Gabriel willingly lifted the rotund silver Persian into his arms and welcomed Sass's heavy, power laden purr, knowing the purpose of it and letting it in as I'd learned to. "And no matter what happens, we do what we do because it's the right thing."

"The only thing." Gabriel buried his nose in Sass's fur. "I want to go home, Mom."

The house. His old room. I saw it in his mind. And opened the way to the kitchen while my mind tried to decipher more from my conversation with Nona so I didn't have to think about more painful things.

What if Trill knew what the pieces would do? That almost pulled me to a halt. What if she diverted the arm because its return would trigger something we weren't ready for? A chain of events kind of thing? I stepped out into the warmth of late afternoon and into the power of the coven as that epiphany hit. That would make sense. Though the fact we didn't feel ready for any of this wasn't lost on me. Still. It fit, right?

I needed to talk to Max. If Trill was controlling the order of the return of the pieces...

But why? Who told her? Maybe Zoe. Fate had a direct line to Creator. That would tie things together, right? If that was the case, why not just freaking tell me already? There had to be a reason to keep me in the dark.

If I was right about Trill's role, this changed

everything.

The massive understanding of that thought already in my mind, I rocked back on my heels as Trill's mental touch slammed into mine before I could even close the veil behind me.

She appeared at my side, jerking me free of my son while Gabriel just watched. Sass squeaked a protest and Jiao lunged for me, but too late. I plunged back into the veil, not under my own power, in the control of the one person in the Universe I wasn't sure I could trust.

EIGHTEEN

I almost fought her. Would have, just a little while ago, before the encounter in the chapel in Sanctuary. Instead, at war inside about who she was and what that might mean, I let her take me deep into the veil before reaching out to speak to her.

Trill. I carefully kept judgement and anger from my mental voice. *I need to know what's going on.*

She didn't answer that particular question, instead pulling to a halt and pointing below us. She'd formed some kind of window in the veil and I felt compelled to follow her gesturing index finger with my gaze even as I wondered how she managed such a feat.

How much had she changed from the girl I used to know?

The moment I looked into the window, we were falling together, though when we emerged through the other side I knew it wasn't like passing through the veil. I felt insubstantial, almost ghostlike. As if my consciousness had made the trip without my body.

And almost leaped from my skin when I turned to see a tall, scowling demon staring back at me. I knew her, had seen her this way only once before. When she'd left my body and I feared she'd never return. She wasn't alone, the slim, worried form of Shaylee waving meekly at me. But it was the cold, pale appearance of the vampire essence, her icy white eyes and hair wavering softly around her that shook me the most.

Ladies, she sent, nodding to Trill who watched us with her lower lip clamped between her teeth.

I'm sorry, she sent. *I forgot you're not just you.* She shrugged, hands flexing before she stilled again. *I hope this is okay.*

As long as you can put us all back again, my demon snarled, her black horns sparking with amber fire.

I'm sure that's the case, Shaylee sent. *Isn't it, Trill?*

Of course. Confidence. As long as it wasn't an act.

Odd to see you this way, my vampire sent, a faint smile on her lips. Her skin was completely white, and without lines, her eyes huge, rimmed in black. She gave me the creeps, honestly, body shimmering with spirit power under the slim fitting white dress she wore.

You too, I sent, clamping my mental teeth together to keep them from chattering. It felt so lonely like this. They were still part of me, of the physical me, but I missed having them in my head.

So weird.

Come. Trill gestured for us to follow and we did, drifting through dark hallways of black stone.

Where are we? I glanced around, not recognizing anything. We weren't on my home plane, or any other that felt familiar. And when we passed a window, I looked out for a landmark. And saw only darkness. Not a moon, a star, nothing in the sky.

This place is protected by Dark Brother and his power. Trill continued moving and I flinched when someone marched toward us. But the tall, slim young man simply walked through my guide and past me as I hastily moved aside. *This is the only way we can penetrate Belaisle's stronghold.*

Belaisle's—

Yes. My demon's snarl of victory crackled with power as Trill led us around a sharp corner and into a wide, tall ceilinged room that ached with darkness. But even that black couldn't disguise the shining pieces resting on the stone dais. Even through the shroud of sorcery meant to keep them safe, the foot and ear of Creator glowed with the power of She who made them.

A mix of excitement and terror washed over me. *Why the sudden hurry?* And why was Trill helping us now? Unless I was right and she'd somehow ended up the one who decided when and where the pieces were returned.

You must bring these back to Creator. Trill's hands shook, her body vibrating with tension she hadn't shown before. Her head lowered and when she looked back up again she had regained control.

Belaisle is here, isn't he? Of course he was. And I could put an end to this once and for all.

Let's go find out. My demon turned, ready to tear him apart with her spirit alone. But Trill's sharp cry stopped her, stopped all of us.

Please, you have to listen. She took a breath, though I was sure her soul didn't technically need to breathe. *There is a time and a place for everything.*

An order, I said, feeling my own chest tighten. Or that's how it came across. Did my soul have a chest? Too confusing to worry about.

Exactly. She gave great weight to that word, staring me down a moment before going on. My vampire tilted her head to the right, observing with her cool calculation.

He has a role to play as much as we do. She had to say that, didn't she? Guaranteeing I'd give up my plans to turn him into mush?

Grumble, mumble.

If you pursue him here, now, Trill sent with the same intensity, *things won't end the way you think they will, Doombringer.* Ack. That again. I suppressed the chill that made me shudder, saw even my demon rub her arms as if to ward off goosebumps. *The order must be obeyed.*

As in the Order, Dark Brother's soldiers? Now I was confused. The play on words made my head ache. *They are part of this?*

I believe your original supposition is correct. My vampire turned from Trill to me. *It is she who commands the correct order of return of the pieces.* Trill flinched slightly, didn't respond. But she'd given me my answer without having to.

The other side is cheating. Trill shivered, shook her head. *I'm not sure why Zoe is helping them, but she's not supposed to. This is between—*

Enough! Right on cue, Fate appeared, silencing Trill with a blast of volume and power. The Zornov maji glared back.

I'm doing what Creator asked, she sent, the pair facing off over the pieces. They were expending so much power, crackling around them, the dark pushed back, lighting the stone walls, and surely had to be enough to draw unwanted attention at some point. Still, here was the possibility of answers, right?

If we stay out of it, my vampire sent. *And observe.*

But my original fear was correct. Within seconds of Zoe's appearance, Belaisle came running, a tunnel of black forming beside Shaylee.

Syd! Trill's power pulled me forward and I felt disorientation shove me around. I landed hard on the floor, three personas—four counting my own—stuffed back into my physical body as the Zornov maji jerked me all the way over into this plane. *RUN!*

Belaisle's shocked expression was almost reward enough. And I could have stayed, could have fought him and maybe won. But, this was too important.

And I chose, instead, to trust Trill. Imagine.

With a jaunty wave that mimicked the arrogant toss off he'd often shared with me when in this same position, I leaped bodily through the shields, my white sorcery making an easy hole, and landed on the pieces, opening the veil at the same instant.

And fell through into the darkness beyond with the two chunks of statue pressed to my chest.

Where have you been? The foot snarked at me in a young man's voice as I jerked at the veil for the second time, terror and elation spinning in time with the desperate need to get to safety. *You botched the first recovery. I think I've been waiting long enough.* Right. We'd been together on the frozen plane, just before Trill stole the piece from me on Zoe's insistence. Why did all of the chunks of Creator have such nasty personalities? His whole attitude problem wasn't making things any better.

Oh, hush, the ear muttered, female this time, correcting my assumption the pieces were all asshats. *Can't you see she's busy?*

I laughed. Out loud. Barked it like a madwoman. Couldn't help it as I hit the ground running in the statue chamber of the Stronghold.

You think she's stable? The foot's hissing whisper was so loud it made my head ring.

Really, dear, the ear sent. *You've always been impatient.*

Smartaasses. Just what I needed.

I scrambled up the base of the statue, juggling the foot and ear, my haste making me clumsy and slower than I should have been. But all I could imagine was Belaisle coming after me, pursuing me, taking the precious pieces back. Gabriel was right. Whether the Universe suffered for it or not, I had to replace them.

But that wasn't my job, was it? The moment I stood on Creator's lap, the ear pressed to the side of Her head and not one blessed thing happened—while I muttered to myself the foot would have been a better attempt, wouldn't it?—I understood. My son. I needed my son.

Well, at least she's thinking straight again, the foot sent.

The ear just sighed.

Someone was here. I spun, panic rising, to find Max stepping through the veil, staring up at me with shock on his face.

"Syd?" He paused, gaze traveling over the stone parts clutched haphazardly in my arms before his eyes rose to meet mine again. "Where did you find those?"

I didn't get to answer. And despite not calling him personally, when Gabriel appeared alone, grim faced and determined, I knew I didn't have to.

Finally, the foot griped. *The Gateway.*

At last, the ear sent, joy in her voice. *Home.*

I slipped from Creator's lap, leaving the pieces behind while my son nodded to me on the way by. I could have given him a boost but he didn't need it, his magic lifting him easily into reach. I staggered away, to Max's side, reaching out in a strange need I'd never shared with him before, to hold his hand and take comfort from the touch of another being as my son recreated the one who made this Universe and tore it apart at the same time.

"Mom." Gabriel turned toward me, the ear in one hand, the foot balanced in a net of energy in the other. "Trill?"

I nodded, swallowed. "Trill." Drew a breath. "Sweets, who is she working for?"

He didn't answer, turning as he went back to his task.

This time when the Stronghold shook I just stood there, feeling the veil collapsing, the loss of planes without needing—or wanting—to observe them, Max kindly holding my hand.

And did my part when the two souls of the drach who protected the pieces all this time sang the songs that were their names—a stunning older man Max called uncle and a young female he bowed to with a whispered *cousin* —and rose into the air, waving farewell to the one who had doomed them to this in the first place.

I owed him that much.

NINETEEN

Gabriel came to me, the stranger he'd been gone now, aware and himself all over again. I clung to Max as I hugged my son to me with one arm, feeling empty and alone despite the boy who squeezed me tight and the powerful drach holding my hand.

The world finally settled again, the Stronghold's shaking subsiding, dust filling the air, making me cough.

"Mom," Gabriel whispered into my t-shirt. "I'm sorry."

I shook my head and pushed him gently back, finally releasing Max. The ribbon on my wrist flexed and released its tight hold, sighing in such an accustomed way I almost stared at it. I knew that sigh, but from where? Didn't matter now. I had the grief of my son to deal with.

"Never apologize for doing what has to be done." I looked up at Max, shrugged in a bout of wonder. Three pieces in such a short period of time, after all this searching and guilt and anger. Two thirds of the way there in an eye blink. Seemed anti-climactic. "Now what?"

"I take it from your conversation with Gabriel Trill assisted in the return of the two pieces." Max's calm might have irritated me any other time. But right now it helped me level out, settle, find my own balance in the whirling emotions fighting for control over me. Even Gabriel seemed less hurt, more relaxed as I nodded.

I filled them in on what had happened, shivering a bit at the memory of my alter egos outside me.

Refreshing experience, my vampire sent and I had a flash of her true face, something I'd never had before. I wasn't sure if it would change how I felt about her, now I knew what she looked like. Odd, right?

"You believe it's up to Trill to decide when the pieces are returned." That wasn't a question. The giant drach lord was nodding slowly as if this made immense sense to him. Nice to know I wasn't delusional or anything. "That means the three remaining pieces will find their way to us in due time."

I hated not being in control of things. "She gave me that impression." Maybe I should have been happier knowing events were unfolding as they were meant to. Mostly. "What worries me is Trill's comment about Zoe. And how Fate tried to stop me from taking the pieces." If Trill was working for Creator like Zoe was...

Who did I trust?

"This continuing reference to order concerns me." Max stared up at the statue of Creator. "It smacks of a warning Dark Brother's soldiers will make it through despite our best efforts."

"Or has nothing to do with them," Gabriel said. "Trill's right about order, though."

My head snapped down, eyes boring holes into my eldest. "Young man," I said, "I think it's time you came clean on what you know."

My son flinched, looked away. "Mom," he said, voice breaking. "I can't. I'm sorry." He tossed his hands, a gesture far older than his little body should have been familiar with. "We all have our jobs to do. And this is mine." He glanced back at Creator. "Among other things."

I almost didn't catch that last, but instead of losing my crap as I was about to do, I stood still and held my tongue as Max spoke.

"Let us agree we are on the right path," he said in his kind and stoic way. Grrr. Fine. "You agree, then, Gabriel, that the other side is, as Trill put it, cheating?"

My son's concern showed clearly on his face. Yeah, like mother like kid. "I was supposed to have returned the foot and ear before now." His lips clamped shut, face pale as if he'd given too much away.

Shaking my child was out of the question.

Keep telling yourself that, Syd.

"Sweets." I knelt next to him, stroked my fingers over his cheek with more tenderness than I thought I had in me at the moment. "We need answers."

He hugged me around the neck, pressing his little lips to my ear.

"There's a reason I can feel the pieces," he whispered. "That's my job, Mom."

"Because you're the Gateway." I knew that already.

He leaned back, misery on his face. And shook his head, but the gesture seemed ambiguous. Like there was more to it he wasn't telling me. Not a denial, but not the rest of the story, either. Instead of speaking again or filling me in—because that would be the best way to diffuse me—he simply let me go.

Max's next interruption saved my son from my building tirade yet again.

"Who, then, is influencing Fate if she works against us now?" His deep voice vibrated with concern. There was a time his true love, Bellanca, the Light Fate, was the distant eyes of Creator. Along with her brother, that was. It had to be hard for the drach leader to remember that was no longer the case. The two Fates were removed from that position, both with their physical vision returned to them along with their maji status. Gone forever their ability to see the future.

I wondered suddenly how they were faring. I'd left

them in the care of Iepa, their fellow maji and the only one of that race I trusted. She'd been silent since. I really needed to check in and see if the second race was suffering like the rest of the Universe.

My son stood, mute and miserable, before us.

I had to do something. And since they were on my mind, I'd take the maji as the distraction I needed before I turned the Gateway over onto my knee and spanked him.

Like I'd ever raised an angry hand to my kids. But, as I tore with frustration at the veil, I grumbled to myself there was always a first time.

I landed, Max at my side, Gabriel reluctantly following, in the Fate's chamber by the fountain where once Light Fate had resided. For a brief second I wondered if it was a bad idea bringing my son here. After all, the last time I'd let him come the maji leader, Zeon, had attacked him, showing him the race Gabriel tried to save had died horrible deaths on the new plane he'd relocated them to. Never mind their own plane was dying, them along with it. Gabriel had tried his best. But it had almost broken my son, the fact he'd caused their end instead of the good he'd tried to do.

Too late now. He was with me and no way was I sending him home alone. Besides, within another instant I realized it didn't matter if he was with me or not.

Something was terribly wrong. The last time I'd been

here, the maji were nowhere to be found, but their power at least remained linked to Center. This time? Nada, zilcho, bupkis.

The maji and all the power of the second race were gone.

I gaped into the quiet of the plane while Max's power reached out, seeking what I knew was already missing. I turned in a slow circle, feeling the utter emptiness of Center even as I understood that wasn't quite accurate.

Two souls remained. They appeared at the entry to the grotto, their matching blond hair and pale eyes as well known to me as the drach beside me. But these two who had been Fates of the Universe weren't the people I used to know.

Bellanca's burning bitterness had changed her from the kind, thoughtful young woman she'd appeared to be to a caricature of herself, lines formed around her eyes, her mouth. She'd aged in her resentment, body hunching slightly, still slim and attractive, but no longer pretty. Anger had darkened her and I knew she would never recover from the blame she felt toward Creator for taking away her lifelong task.

And how would I feel if, after millennia, I had such power stripped from me and handed to another with what felt like a casualness that bordered on indifference?

Her brother seemed less the worse for wear, though Thanos was equally altered by this new state of affairs.

Also older in appearance, less a late teen and closer to my age, his lips had pulled into what seemed to be a permanent smirk, his own anger bubbling behind his eyes.

"Where are the maji?" I didn't mean to just blurt out the question, but I was so shocked by the emptiness of Center I couldn't think of anything else to say. Way to be all sensitive to the hurt of others, Syd.

Bellanca shrugged, bitterness coming through her magic, through the tightness of her jaw as it jumped in response. "Gone," she said, as if that told me what I needed to know.

This was terrible. If the second race was already lost to the void... I couldn't even comprehend what that meant. Was the Universe so far gone already?

"They are too strong for the void to have taken them this soon." Max seemed confused, hurt by Bellanca's attitude.

She frowned at him, tossed her head. "Small minded, as always, drach." Where once I'd only ever heard love from her when she spoke to him, now there was pure contempt. "They departed of their own choosing."

"Why?" I must have whispered that word. Though the fact the maji were unwilling, even now, to step up and do something to save the Universe really wasn't that big of a shocker. In fact, the moment the question passed my lips I felt my own anger rise, burning away my shock when Bellanca spoke.

"The blood of the maji will be on your hands." She jabbed one index finger in my direction, body quivering from the force of her gesture. "You call evil down on all of us, Doombringer. And I for one will not remain to see the end." She snapped her fingers with a glare for Max and disappeared into a flare of fire.

Thanos remained behind, his gaze fixed on the spot where his sister had been a long moment before he looked up, the smirk falling from his face. I almost preferred his arrogance over the deep and abiding pain in his eyes.

"My sister," he said, "has become cruel and impatient. And though I understand her hurt, I can only hope Creator knows what She is doing."

I nodded, swallowed down a sharp retort. "Where did the maji go, Thanos?"

"We don't know." He shook his head, hands wringing at his sides. "Their dark brethren have also fled." His people, the ones he'd lived with at Core for so many centuries. Had to hurt, that second betrayal. Going without him like that.

"You're sure they didn't fall into the void?" Max's voice was quiet, but calm still. I knew he had to be in pain from the encounter with Bellanca, but he was as steady as always.

"This place remains," Thanos said, gesturing around

him. "As does Core. Their power is simply gone, away with them."

Right. Every other time we placed a piece, planes had vanished right along with the people and power on them, hadn't they? Except the vampires. And the Order. Neither seemed connected directly to the planes or their disappearance. Both races appeared inclined to just poof out of existence all on their own. Irked me I still didn't know why that was.

"Will you help us?" It seemed a silly question. Especially since there really wasn't much we could do right now. Thanos shook his head, looked away, smirk returned.

"Go, Doombringer," he said. "Ruin everything. And save us all."

With that, he vanished after his sister.

Not much we could do from there. Max led us back to the Stronghold, my son silent beside me. He'd not said a word in what felt like forever, remaining still and quiet through the entire exchange with the old Fates. But, the moment we passed through into the statue chamber, my son shook himself as if he'd just woken from a dream.

"Mom," he said. "I have an idea. But you're not going to like it."

I clamped my lips together and nodded. Chances were if acting meant putting himself at risk, he was right. But who was I to tell the Gateway what he could and couldn't do? His mother, damn it, that's who.

Syd. Hush.

Gabriel glanced at Max then back to me, little shoulders squaring. "I want to send my soul back into the veil."

Reaction #1: Oh, *hell* no.

Reaction #2: OVER MY DEAD BODY.

Reaction #3: Dear Creator, it might be the only way…

"Mom, just listen." He continued to hold my gaze while my stomach turned over and I fought the need to throw up at the memory of his little body, lifeless but for the soft and infrequent da-dum that had been all that remained of his mortal existence. I felt that heartbeat, the recall of it, like a shudder through my body as he went on. "We need the other four pieces. And I can see so much when I'm in there." His eyes took on a faraway expression that terrified me even more.

Da-dum.

Twitch.

"I can find them if I go in, I know it."

Da-dum.

"Just let me try."

Da—

And then, I understood. Like a flash of pain, a hit to my solar plexus, a punch deep into the heart of my soul, I knew why it shook me so much, that sound.

That soft and pathetic da-dum.

Liam.

The last sound I ever heard from him was the final beat of his heart.

It took everything I had in me not to scream, to sob out loud, to grab my son and never, ever let go. Rigid with the need to keep myself from flying apart, I clenched my entire being into a rapidly stiffening plank of HELL TO THE NEVER and shook my head.

"I forbid you to go," I said.

Fury flared in the child before me, rage like I'd only ever seen a few times before. Felt myself an instant or two along the way. But never, ever in my son.

Gabriel clenched both hands at his sides, power pulsing out beneath him, shaking the ground at my feet, before he snarled in response.

"We'll see," he snapped, creating a narrow Gateway and leaving without another word. It slammed shut behind him before I could cross into his bedroom in Wilding Springs, to follow him home. At least he went home. Still, he'd walked away from me during a fight.

Oh, no he did *not*.

Syd. Mom had perfect timing. If perfect meant the worst freaking choice of moments ever known to the Universe in all time and space.

WHAT. Yikes, Syd. Really?

Bless her, Mom knew better than to fight fire with

nuclear armaments, though the singe of anger in her mental voice told me she was holding back by the skin of her teeth.

Sweetheart. She paused an instant as I pulled my crap together and didn't lose it again on her.

Mother. Okay, that was better, more civil. Kinda.

I hate to interrupt, she sent, tight and precise. *But we've been summoned.*

Really. I caught myself in mid-grind, forced my teeth apart through sheer willpower. I was going to live forever. I'd be needing my molars a few centuries from now. *By whom?*

You're going to love this. Her voice growled in my head. *Tallah and Sashenka Hensley have brought a grievance against us to the World Paranormal Council. Our presence is requested to face charges.*

They *what?* The lying, deceitful, arrogant—

I grinned tightly into the empty air. A fight. How perfect. And just what I needed.

I'm on my way.

TWENTY

Mom was waiting for me when I arrived at Harvard to pick her up. She looked about as impressed by the summons as I was, bracketed by two lurking, black hounds with new white fire in their eyes. Good to see she'd taken my advice. Now the earth magic had gone, they should have vanished with it. But their new power kept them grounded and out of the veil with the rest of the Sidhe, it seemed. Made me wonder in a flash if I should make sure every race had access to white sorcery. Would it keep them safe?

To what end, though? All it would do would be put off the inevitable. I was glad the hounds were here to have Mom's back. But everyone else would just have to trust Creator knew what She was doing putting the fate of the Universe in my hands.

It would be laughable if it wasn't so terrifying.

I was still in a cranky mood, about as happy as my son when I popped into Wilding Springs to finish my fight with Gabriel. Told his closed bedroom door to behave and left him at home with Sassafras and a command to stay the hell in his own body and out of the veil.

"I thought you had Tallah in custody." Came out like an accusation. First words out of my mouth used as weapons? Nailed it.

Mom's jaw tightened, Darae whining softly in sympathy. At least my mother could afford to wear her teeth down. She only had one lifetime to worry about. "The WPC," she snarled out the term before visibly pulling herself into her diplomatic Miriam Hayle persona and continuing in cold fluidity, "divested us of the pair of Hensley's shortly after we arrived." I bet that went over well. Would have liked to see Quaid face down my mother with that order.

He won though, didn't he? Despite the two lurking dogs. I knew why, of course. Their power was gone, their earth magic, at least. Though Mom's choice to share the white sorcery with them—the source of their new eye tint—meant they were far from helpless. In fact, they felt stronger than ever. I ignored them as they remained silent, watchful.

Oddly, despite the setback, Varity seemed the only one of our collective in a good mood. She should have been pissed off, right? Her authority challenged and all that crap. When I scowled at her, she winked back.

"You two have no idea," she chortled, rubbing her long, thin hands together in unconcealed glee, "how long I've been looking forward to a Hayle family tag team."

Oh, dear.

On the other hand, I agreed with her. It was far past time to deal with Femke, no matter what that took. Mom's power simmered beside me, the young magic of the new North American Witches Council bubbling with its need to prove itself. Was my mother feeling the same way? She had nothing to prove, not after all the successes and accomplishments she'd managed over the years.

Made me wonder, though, calmed me down a little bit as we passed out of the veil and into the main council meeting room in Hong Kong. Mom had to be struggling with her decisions as much as I did.

Nice to know we were still peas in a pod.

I wasn't sure if the small gathering we strode forward to join was a good sign or a bad one. With Galleytrot and Darae in our midst, we almost outnumbered the waiting official party of Femke, Tallah, Sashenka, Quaid and two Enforcers standing guard at the door. I might have preferred the full assemblage of the WPC to witness what was about to happen instead of just the Hensley sisters who scowled at us with the same unhappiness that shone on Femke's face.

Minus the insanity I saw behind her eyes. She had to be nuts to think such a small group could stand against me. Hell, that her entire Enforcer order even had a chance. Damn it, I'd left this too long. No more. I'd find out what was wrong with my friend, what the Russians did to her, and fix her if it was the last thing on my list.

Quaid stood off to one side, eyes dark, hooded, magic tight and guarded. No help there, though he'd asked me in the past to save his boss from herself. Maybe he couldn't assist, but hopefully he'd at least stay out of the way when the time came. Because there was a giant fight brewing, that much was certain.

And the focus of the thundercloud stared at me with open hatred in her empty, dark eyes.

"I demand you arrest them both." Tallah looked quite a bit worse for wear, her long, silky hair no longer a fall of perfection but knotted and greasy on the ends, hanging more like a shroud than a proud banner of her heritage. Her dark skin had taken on a gray cast, lines and circles deep around her big eyes bulging wider with her distress, pulling down the corners of her full mouth. The loss of her family magic hit her hard, clearly. I could attest to how it felt, though mine I'd shed on purpose, admittedly, and not had it torn from me unwillingly.

Had to hurt.

Compassion might serve us best, my vampire sent.

Like hell. My demon's anger burned in the pit of my

stomach while Shaylee sighed.

No matter what happens here, she sent, her own soul weighted and dark, *we must do what we can to save Femke.*

Right. No losing sight of the prize. Freeing the WPC leader of whatever held her in thrall had to be the priority. Prodding my Sidhe princess and her low ego would have to wait until I was done.

I'm fine, she sent privately, sadly. *Just missing the feeling of earth magic, Syd. Don't you?*

I came to a halt next to Mom, testing for truth I knew already. When I examined those around me, I confirmed they, too, were empty of that most base of magicks. The strain and stress in their faces, the way they twitched from the lowest Enforcer to the way Femke's cheek vibrated as she shifted in her position before us, gave me a flash of insight.

Everything that was happening here, all the strife and conflict, was tied to the fact they'd lost something precious. Were they aware of it? I had to believe they were. Or, maybe they weren't and their confrontational angst was a reaction to how deeply it affected them.

Mom, I sent in a tight thought as she addressed Femke formally. I didn't hear her specific words, didn't need to. Some kind of politico speak to appease the history makers, likely. *You do know your earth magic is gone, right?*

She glanced sideways at me, body jerking just a little. *Yes*, she sent, her own distress growing as her power grappled for what was no longer there. *I'm aware. This is relevant now?* I shared my epiphany and she sighed mentally. *First spirit and now earth?* I knew panic in her when I heard it, though others might only sense concern. *Syd, what's happening?*

You know what's happening. And it's changing the way we react to each other. Or how individuals without those powers did, at least. I was one of the lucky ones.

Us too, Shaylee whispered.

Femke and the others stared at us, Tallah quivering, waiting for us to say something. But this was important. Let them think we were at a loss for words or conspiring against them.

Understood, Mom sent, voice quavering. *So we can expect more of this, then?* How did she hold in such fear? I loved my mother so much. But I owed it to her to be blunt.

The spirit magic left. Earth followed. The others will go in turn, Mom, until there's no power left.

Now panic did show in her eyes and it almost killed me, because it was so vivid. Mom never panicked. But, as I shrugged internally, I showed her the white sorcery, reminded her of its presence. We might lose that which was the most familiar, but so far the new power of Creator didn't seem effected by the return of Her pieces. Hopefully we'd be left at least that in the end.

If I had to face the destruction of the Universe, surely it wouldn't be as a powerless normal.

Shudder.

Mom settled and nodded back as her natural instinct to serve and protect kicked in, returning to the task at hand as if we'd never had this little conversation on the side.

Go, Mom.

"The autonomy of individual councils has held for as long as we've had territories," Mom said, voice steady, casual. My respect for her arched into the stratosphere. No way would I have been able to pull off that kind of professionalism in face of what I'd just told her. Or in front of these glaring, judging faces. In fact, a few choice swears sat in the back of my mind courtesy of my demon—yeah, we'll blame her—while Mom handled things.

"And yet it wasn't your council that handed down sentence," Femke snarled, hand shaking when it clamped down on her opposite wrist as if in effort to still her palsy. I glanced over Tallah's shoulder, seeing the flat anger on Shenka's face as she glared her own hate past her sister. Let her. She'd earned this. "You sent a rogue witch and who knows what else to deal with it."

"No." Okay, I was so done it wasn't even funny. How many times had I stood in front of people like this who had no freaking clue what was really going on and took their abuse through trying to be diplomatic? Done.

Not the response they were expecting. Tallah

flinched, a moment of fear in her eyes. I almost smiled out of sheer frustration.

"You must answer for what you've done." Femke's tone of voice shuddered, her pale, blue eyes widening to mimic the former Hensley leader's. Spittle foam formed in the corners of her mouth, the shaking of her body increasing. She looked like a cartoon character about to explode, her power as out of control as she appeared to be. Everonus claimed he'd kept her under wraps, and now I saw for my own eyes he'd been telling me the truth. I realized then, as I examined her, exactly why my ex-husband was so rigid and quiet. Only Quaid's magic managed to curb her now. And I wasn't sure how much longer he'd be able to keep her contained.

Syd, Galleytrot's rumbling voice echoed in my head, sounding less like a spring thunderstorm now his earth power was gone and more like an encroaching hurricane. *We'll protect Miriam. End this.* Darae's answering growl supported him.

Okay then. Relief washed through me. I didn't realize I'd been worried about my mother, about bringing her here with her magic diminished despite the white sorcery in her possession. But with these two at her back, I could act and know Mom would be safe.

"I'd like to know," Mom said, interrupting my conversation with the hounds and the rude and obvious response my demon was forming in answer to Femke, "how two criminals from my territory ended up here in the custody of the WPC." True that. Leave it to my mother to remain focused on the important details.

Quaid flinched. "I removed Tallah Hensley to Hong Kong under direct orders." There was an apology to Mom in his voice. Varity snorted next to me. I'm sure I imagined the soft tendrils of smoke emerging from her nostrils when she did.

"Without permission to enter my territory." It was the Enforcer leader who snapped at him.

He didn't respond. He was far too busy containing Femke.

I reached out with energy to support him but he slapped me away.

Just help her. Even his mental voice sounded strained. *I'll hold her together. But I can't act against her, Syd. You have to figure out what the hell is wrong and fix it.*

No hints? He had to know something if he was this close to her magic.

No freaking clue. That amount of frustration had to be tearing him apart. As did asking for my help when he knew damned well the reason he left me in the first place was to prove he didn't need me.

Okay then.

"I was accused and tried and sentenced by one without the right to do so." Whatever, Tallah. Keep lying to yourself, sister. She jabbed a finger at me. "Without the right to present my case."

I'd had enough of this crap. Mind crackling fury, I reached for Piers even as I snarled at her. The white power of the two hounds woke, circling my mother, their protections perhaps unnecessary but freeing me to act without worry Femke might try to seize Mom and use her against me. I'd like to see her try to get past the furious, growling black dogs. "Fine," I said, feeling him respond instantly. "Let's have your case presented, Tallah. Right now." A black tunnel opened and Piers appeared, gray longcoat swinging in time with his knee length blond hair. The hunched, furious form of the former Brotherhood leader he had in his power looked far less sure of himself.

Tallah flinched visibly and backed up a half step. Even Shenka seemed to cool off, guilt on her face.

"What's the matter, Hensleys?" I had the bit in my teeth despite Mom's hissing for me to shut the hell up. "You asked for the chance to defend yourselves. So do it." I jerked Jean Marc forward with my own power, Piers's helping eagerly. "Tell us how you aligned with the Brotherhood and how you planned to betray all witches again out of your own stupidity and need for power. Tell us, Tallah."

She wouldn't look at me, face flat and dark.

"This is insane." Bad choice of words? Maybe, but that's what it felt like. I released Jean Marc, Piers taking over again. He had the good sense to remain silent, though from the tightness of his lips he was doing his best not to grin in triumph.

"You will release Jean Marc Dumont to me." Femke staggered as one knee gave slight way, but she righted herself immediately. Her power swirled in response, the WPC magic reacting violently to her mood swing. I was positive everyone in the room felt it, from the way they stared at her like she'd bitten them. I hit Quaid hard with magic, white sorcery feeding his power.

He didn't argue this time, sweat standing out on his upper lip. He'd lost the invisible support of Everonus. Had to be hitting him hard. Alone, there was no way he'd last.

Damn it, I'm taking her down, Mom. It was the only way.

No. My mother's denial hit me like a blow. *You can't, Syd. If you act against Femke publically, like this, there will be war. And whether you like it or not, they won't be able to come after you. So they'll come after me.*

Mom didn't look at me. She didn't have to. She was right.

Galleytrot howled his frustration, the massive windows shuddering as thunder clapped outside the high rise in response to his protest.

Okay, so maybe I couldn't take her down. But I now had access to her power through my tie to Quaid. Time to find out what the hell was going on inside her.

TWENTY-ONE

It was Piers who spoke while I dove into Femke's magic and started digging. "The Steam Union has full jurisdiction over this prisoner," he said, as calm as my mother. I really had to take lessons from the two of them on how to hide my feelings behind that kind of precision. "Any attempt the WPC makes to liberate him from our possession will be seen as an act of war." And his temper was showing. So maybe he wasn't the best one to teach me after all.

Didn't matter. I was swimming in a cesspool of magic so torn and damaged I could barely breathe. I only peripherally heard the rest of the exchange. Femke barked ineffectual and contradictory orders while Mom did her best to diffuse the situation. Quaid shivered beside me, around me, following me deep into Femke who didn't seem to notice we were even there.

Nothing. No trace of what had been done to her, not a hint or a spark or a—

There. A flicker, on the edge of the maelstrom. I dove for it, grasped it. Fell into memory—

—*being beaten by Nickolay Vetrov, agony as my magic is torn from me, manipulated by sorcery, crushed and reassembled, forced back into my body*—

—*hazy reality, colors kaleidoscoping around me, voices I barely hear, pressure on my soul as I weep inside for the hurt that hums constantly under everything*—

—*one hope permeating everything, a face, a voice I adore, she'll come for me, she'll never rest until I'm free*—

I flinched back from my own face hovering in that memory. Femke's last hope was me. And I failed her.

No, Quaid sent, sharp and insistent. *Syd, look.*

Deeper then, experience all of it. I owed my friend that much. I dove back in—

—*knowing she's coming, feeling her near despite all of it, laughing through the drug while the small, insane man with the black power slices through my magic and implants himself there*—

I was thrown from Femke's mind and power, staggering slightly, head on fire for an instant before my vampire soothed it. And felt my stomach clench into a knot so tight I could barely draw breath.

That's why, my demon sent, her normal fire cooled in her anxiety.

Poor Femke. Shaylee wept softly, though her strength

165

never waned.

We must help her. My vampire's anger showed rarely, but now was an appropriate time. Except as I pulled myself back to the present and into the chaos around me, I realized this might be the worst time after all.

Mom's magic vibrated around her as Femke's tried to pin her down. The two hounds repelled the WPC leader's attempt to hold my mother, their own massive capacity filled beyond the magic they'd once controlled. I think I'd made a pair of monsters. Good thing they were on our side. Quaid looked so pale I thought he'd pass out at any moment. Piers had at some point crushed Jean Marc to the floor under a blanket of black and was trying to keep Tallah off his prisoner while Varity held off the other Enforcers.

What the hell happened? Best guess, while I was digging around in her damaged and possessed psyche, Femke snapped.

Might be a good time to interfere, Piers sent to me. *Before someone dies.* He didn't sound amused now. Or like he was kidding.

My white sorcery, tying easily into the black hounds, shut them all down. I hated to do it, but there was no alternative. Heavy handedness wasn't exactly something I shied from, but things were so out of control right now I feared this little act of mine might put Mom at risk as she feared.

No way around it, sweetheart, Mom sent, desperation counterpoint to her grim tone. *I hope you found out something you can use. Because this isn't going to end well if Femke isn't dealt with.*

Oh, I knew what was wrong now. Trouble was, I had no idea how to help. I stared at Femke who thrashed in my grip, teeth chattering with her need to fight me, and tried not to weep with Shaylee.

Konstantin. The damned Black Soul sorcerer. He'd embedded a part of his soul in my friend to control her and it was slowly eating her alive.

Mom, I sent. *Be prepared for anything.* It was all the warning I had to give, opened to Piers and Varity at the same time, to Quaid. The black dogs already linked to me knew the score. Screw everyone else, including the Hensleys. If this went wrong, there was a good chance they'd be mental smears on the floor when I was done.

White sorcery curved into a tight blade, the former hounds of the Wild Hunt backing me, I dove back inside Femke and began to carve away the soul of Konstantin.

Slippery, oily and sneaking past my every move, the slice of black soul evaded me like a snake in the water. What was meant to be a sudden and instant rescue became a long drawn battle where my physical eyes watched Femke's body stretch upward as if she'd been put in a noose, whole body shaking from the effort I made to free her from the slavery of the Black Soul.

Internally Galleytrot and Darae both snapped and snarled at the creeping sliver of spirit, their dog instincts driving them mad with frustration as they chased it down only to fail over and over. They grunted in my mind, whining their frustration. I knew the feeling intimately.

Tallah and Shenka fell back from Femke while the two dogs and I struggled to catch the illusive stain, staring in horror. The room flooded with Enforcers, battering against Varity and Mom and Piers. My determination paled to hope, spun to despair and, finally, as Femke collapsed with the spirit of the evil sorcerer still inside her, failure.

I'm sorry, Syd, Galleytrot panted. *This is beyond us.*

I slammed everyone back, panting, chest hurting as my friend collapsed onto the floor. Dying. The Black Soul was killing her and it would finish the job if I fought against it any longer. It made that infinitely clear to me, the scrap of who Konstantin had been giggling his evil glee into the darkness he spread over her again.

I had all the power in the Universe, skills and experience no one else had. The will and drive to succeed born of hard knocks and steady success against all odds. But right here, right now, when it seemed to matter most, there was nothing I could to do save her. And that hurt most of all.

I let Mom feel it even as I flexed my power and shoved the invading Enforcers out of the room and into the hall, sealing it the door behind them. The two hounds reinforced my shielding, the weight of their massive magic an immobile mountain. Let the Enforcers batter against such power, wear themselves out. It didn't matter, none of it mattered. I'd failed my friend from the moment I let her be kidnapped.

If Konstantin was still alive, I would have killed him myself for what he'd done.

Can we raise his ego and... my demon trailed off. *Oh.*

Yeah. Oh. All of the dead are gone. I hated to sound so pathetic, so without hope. But it was true. Any chance we had of talking to the echo of Konstantin was lost to the void along with the Universe's spirt magic. Maybe I could reach the piece of spirit left behind? Expose it somehow to the void and let that dark place do the rest? But from his original, gleeful retreat, convincing the actual soul of the creature to put itself in a risk situation would actually be harder than leaning on his ego. At least the echo of who he had been would be malleable. The soul, on the other hand... spirits were another matter altogether. And it had anchored to Femke so deeply it was part of her now, linked firmly to her own spirit, keeping itself safe from the pull of the void.

Did anyone really have any experience with this kind of thing? I didn't. The souls I knew—aside from Liam's sacrifice—were long gone after their bodies were dead. There had to be a way.

Can you help? My question to the vampire inside me was tentative and she answered with equal reticence.

I don't know, Syd. Her whisper sounded hoarse and wobbly. *Maybe. But the trouble is containing the spirit inside her. Tracking it and controlling it so it doesn't kill her while we talk to it. I'm not even sure where to start. And trying to expose it to the void might put me at risk. Though it's one I'm willing to take if it will save her life.*

Not even going there.

So now what? My demon wasn't about to let me give up.

We must be practical about this, my vampire sent, soft and regretful. *We may be forced to remove Femke from power so she can no longer be a threat to others.* No mention of the threat she posed to herself.

You mean kill her.

I do. Caring in her tone, but truth. *If that's what we must do.*

No way. There had to be a solution I was missing because I was so emotionally attached, so deep into this. I was just tired. Something would come to me.

Wouldn't it?

"Syd." And then Femke spoke, her blue eyes clear if full of pain, one hand rising toward me. I fell to my knees at her side, cradling her head in my lap. "Oh, Syd. I know. Please, if you love me."

I nodded, tears falling to splash on her pale cheek.

"I'm doing everything I can," I said. "We'll fix this."

"No, Syd," she whispered, the madness creeping in around the edges. "You know what you have to do."

She understands, my vampire sent.

Absolutely *not*. "I'm not killing you," I said.

"Put me out of my misery." Femke wept, shook, pressed her face into my leg. "Please, it hurts so much." Her blue eyes blinked slowly, huge and bulging as she visibly fought what returned to take her over. "I beg you, if you are my friend, my sister," her hand clutched at me, "you will end this now and save all of us from what I'm becoming."

I held her against me, choking on tears that didn't seem to want to stop. *I can't*, I sent. *But I'll save you, Femke. I promise. You just need to hold it together a little while longer. Can you do that?*

Her mental wail drove a dagger of guilt through my heart.

TWENTY-TWO

At least the Enforcers we finally let back in the room didn't try to arrest us outright. Femke regained enough of herself to tell them to stand down, though as I helped her to her feet, shaking and weak, I felt her losing her battle all over again.

We left her in Quaid's care before the black spirit inside her could turn her against us and make this whole mess worse than it already was, fleeing from Hong Kong. Piers left on his own, Jean Marc still in his possession, at least. I trusted him not to let the former Dumont go even if Femke broke completely and came for him. Piers was smart enough to find a way to hide the former Brotherhood leader from her when she recovered.

If she recovered. If the Black Soul inside her hadn't done so much damage to her by now she wouldn't even be able to mumble the alphabet while she drooled in a corner. I should have done what she asked, should have released her from her pain. But Quaid's power and eyes and fear begged me not to and I just couldn't be the one to stop her heart.

I couldn't quit on her no matter what she wanted.

As for Tallah and Shenka, I was all for taking their sorry asses back to Harvard with us, but Mom just shrugged and turned her back on them. There had been no backlash from my workover of Femke thanks to Quaid, so the two remained intact, at least. But they both looked lost, broken, especially when Femke ordered them taken from her presence.

Let them suffer for their choices and try to justify to themselves what they'd done.

Mom sighed in my head as we departed, the cool, dimness of her office in Boston embracing us like a hug after the insanity of the last fifteen minutes. Was it really that short of a time? I shook my head as I sealed the veil behind us, Varity collapsing into a chair across from Mom's desk. "You two know how to throw a party," she said. "I take it we're going to take steps to protect our territory from now on?"

Mom, grim, nodded. "Seal our borders," she said, regret in her eyes. "From all comers."

Not good. But I hardly blamed her. *Do you need my help?* I knew she did and yet, when she hugged me gently, kissing my cheek, she let me go with her heart as much as her body when she stepped away.

"Go," she said. "Do Syd things. We'll handle this."

I grimaced. *Just call*, I sent. *I'm here, Mom.*

I know, sweetheart, she sent. *But I'm also acutely aware now of your other activities.* She winced slightly. *The loss of my power… and the loss of you for six months.* From her tone both were unbearable, brought tears to my eyes I blinked away. She heaved a sigh, as though accepting at last who I'd become. *We need you out there, too. And we'll be fine.*

She didn't sound convinced herself she had things handled, not completely, but I knew better than to argue with her. Loved her for her faith in me, even when my own was on shaky ground.

I left them with a plan half formed in my head, chest tight and sore as I touched down on the grass outside the entrance to the werepalace. Charlotte's magic bumped into mine the moment I appeared, welcoming me inside. I wasn't sure she'd be home, but was glad to find her in her quarters, settling into a soft couch a few minutes later with a glass of wine in my hand and my werewolf royal friends sitting across from me, intent canine senses focused completely.

I loved that about them.

Charlotte didn't flinch when I told them what I'd discovered about Femke, though her husband, Sage, seemed less stoic. He'd not been a werewolf his whole life, so I had to forgive him his lack of complete calm when it came to bad news. That distinction was reserved for the level and dedicated werewoman I knew so well.

When I finished, I took a sip of wine. "I need to see Danilo," I said.

That time I got to her. Charlotte's blue eyes tightened a moment before she sat back, crossing her long legs. "He's in prison." Dull and dead, her tone. So Charlotte.

"I know," I said. "WPC prison. Do you know where?"

She shook her head, but not as a negative. "I'm not sure what you think he can do for you."

"Danilo was in close contact with the mafia at the time Femke was kidnapped," I said. "He might know if there are other Black Soul sorcerers who survived." It was my last hope. If so, if I could track one of Konstantin's people, maybe I could convince him or her to help me.

With violence, if necessary. I hoped it was necessary. Please, let me hit something.

Charlotte's lips twitched, but she nodded sharply, once. "I'm coming with you."

I'd counted on that.

We left the anxious and unhappy Sage behind as my werefriend and I stepped through the veil. *Now what?* Her mental touch always felt more wolfish than woman.

Part of the reason I hoped you'd come, I sent. *You and your brother have the same parents, the same DNA. I might be able to track him through that family connection.*

She held still as I dove into her power, as clear and open to me as always. The wolf in her welcomed me, quiet and watchful. I would never betray its trust, asking it to kindly show me where her brother was. How odd, the way she felt now. There was a time she'd been not quite so perfect, before she embraced her wolf and became whole. I liked her this way much better. She almost felt drach.

Which made me pause. *Have any of your people gone missing?*

Not yet, she sent. *Though I've heard from Piers he's starting to lose sorcerers. And your mother admitted some witch families have vanished.*

Neither of them shared that with me, I growled.

You have more important things to worry about, she sent. *Can you stop the exodus?*

No. Hated admitting it, too.

Then why should they trouble you with obvious issues you can't change? Wolf logic. I could choke her for it sometimes. *Can we get on with this?*

Fine. Whatever.

Femke or Quaid or whoever it was that imprisoned Danilo might have thought they were clever using sorcery to hide him. But they hadn't counted on the combination of Charlotte's still intense connection to her brother—emotional and physical—and the fact my white sorcery trumped their black every day of the week.

We touched down underground in a quiet, white painted hallway with buzzing lights overhead and a sterile scent to the air. Why was it always underground? All the better to crush the souls of those within, I guess. No sight of outside, nothing but the white and the stillness and that horrible smell.

It had to be hell for a werewolf. I'd always thought Mom did Danilo a disservice by letting him live. This would be a fate worse than death for the former wereking. From the sudden flash of despair in Charlotte's wolf magic, she agreed with me, though it was there and gone so fast anyone else would have missed it.

"We should hurry." Her voice barely carried in the muffled air of the hallway. Who knew what the surveillance in this place was like? Chances are whoever guarded this place—Enforcers, more than likely—already knew we were here. Let them try to stop me from seeing Danilo.

From doing what I feared I needed to help Femke. I just hoped I could live with the consequences of what I was about to do.

If Charlotte suspected she didn't say anything, simply led me with unerring confidence across the narrow hall to the white door with the large number 213 on it. Cell number? Who knew? Who cared? Not when it opened at the touch of her hand and she let herself in.

I clenched my jaw against the sight within, the tall,

handsome man with the heavy black beard that reminded me more of a bear than a wolf, who gazed at us from where he sat crossed legged on the floor, looking up with sad eyes.

"I knew you'd come," Danilo said. "I'm ready."

TWENTY-THREE

Was he really? I didn't think so. Sudden anger woke inside me, the same instant power hit my shields. The Enforcers were coming, an alarm claxon sounding overhead as a bright, red light burst into life on the ceiling.

Danilo looked suddenly confused, Charlotte lunging gracefully forward to grasp his arm and jerk him to his feet. So, she did know why we'd come. As she turned with her brother in her grasp, gaze flat and unemotional, I thanked her silently for trusting me.

"I don't think you're ready for this," I said, opening the veil as the magic of four Enforcers hit the door behind us.

"What are you doing?" Panic washed over his face. "I thought you were here to kill me."

Charlotte snorted and shoved him ahead of her

through the gap in the veil. "You're an idiot," she winked at me. "This is a jail break."

Five seconds later we stood on the peak in Nepal, the empty and looming castle of the Empress of vampires watching over us. It was the most remote place I could think of and without any power or observers we could at least have a moment to talk. I locked us down under a shield of white sorcery and crossed my arms over my chest while Danilo shivered, hugging himself under his thin, cream jumpsuit.

He'd lost weight, his usually buff physique now lean and long, making him seem less lumbering juggernaut and sharper blade. Pale skin made him appear wasted, though a terrible hope burned in his dark eyes.

"I don't deserve my freedom." And yet, he wasn't really arguing with me. Charlotte punched him hard in the shoulder, irritation showing.

"Shut up and listen," she snarled.

He nodded, swallowed. "What do you need?"

So willing and eager. I'd take it. And filled him in on what happened up to now. He listened as he shivered in the cold air and I finally took pity on him, warming the bubble we stood inside to a more comfortable temperature while he absorbed what I said.

"You could have asked Mother," he said at last. "She was as much a part of this as I was."

"We know that," I said. "But I figured you had more

incentive to help us than her." And considering she was long gone, escaped through sorcerous assistance to who knew where, I couldn't ask Olena such pressing questions.

Not until I tracked her down and forced the truth from her. Another time. When I had time.

"I don't have proof," he said at last, "but I always suspected the Black Souls infiltrated further into the mafia than just a power connection."

"You mean some of them are in the leadership?" Charlotte chewed her bottom lip a moment. "That actually makes a lot of sense."

It did to me, too. And gave me hope I shouldn't have allowed a place in my heart again. "Can you find out details?" I could go tracking them, of course I could. I'd sworn Femke was a priority. But the disappearance of sorcerers and witches wasn't lost on me and I worried the other massive things on my plate were running off to play without supervision.

I really needed to clone myself.

"I assure you," Danilo said, suddenly intense and a fraction of his old self. "I intend to return to the prison cell or accept my death when this is over." His dark eyes burned. "I am guilty, Sydlynn Hayle. But if helping you and Femke can in some way make a difference, if I can do this to appease the memory of my loving wife," he choked a moment before going on, "I am at your disposal until the end."

Werewolf devotion. Seriously.

"I'm coming with you." Charlotte's grim determination was so like her brother I just sighed.

"The two of you be careful." I could have sent Danilo alone, I knew that to the bottom of my toes. His word was enough, his aching need to prove himself and his faithfulness written all over him. But knowing Charlotte would be with him made me feel this might actually work out. Never mind she was the werequeen. I knew better than to tell her to stay home and be a good wolf girl. Instead, I reached out, took her hand and shared the power I'd been handing out lately. Her eyes widened but she accepted without comment, the white sorcery bonding visibly to the lychos she'd become like they were made for each other.

Charlotte shivered, delight on her face a moment before she settled again and shrugged at me, hand on her brother's arm. "We'll be in touch."

I opened the shielding and let them go. She had more than enough power to protect them and the white sorcery I'd just given her meant an added level up.

They'd be fine. And would get the information I needed. Now, back to my regularly scheduled Universe saving.

And how was that going for me? Don't ask.

SYD! Why did someone shouting my name in my

head always make me leap and act? Probably because the people in my life who did so only called for help when they were desperate.

Awesome.

Sass. I was in the veil already, felt a twinge of something that made me pause, even as the cat's mental voice slammed hard against me again, his magic showing me a vision that made my heart stop beating.

My son. On the floor of his bedroom. Empty eyes staring at the ceiling.

GABRIEL! I screamed his name into the veil. Because, of course, I knew exactly what my child had done.

You don't have to yell, Mom, he sent, quite calm and composed as he spoke through the veil to me like abandoning his body to join with the Universe was no big deal.

Fury warred with fear did a cha-cha with pride as I pulled myself together in mid-leap for Wilding Springs. I hugged his soul to me, but he slipped free this time, not allowing me to jerk him out of the veil. Instead, his spirit danced away, almost joyful while I panted pure terror into the dimness.

Come home this instant. Yeah, like ordering one of the Universe's most powerful beings to go to his room was going to get me anywhere. I had to have kids, didn't I?

This is the only way, Mom, and you know it. I'll be back soon.

And then, Gabriel was gone.

Fuming, I stepped through into his room, finding Sass in cat form huddled in a miserable ball in Jiao's arms, his ears hanging sideways, whiskers drooping low. It wasn't his fault, or hers. But saying so wouldn't help.

I knew that from experience myself. Self-blame was a family curse.

The only activity in the room came from the colored ribbons that bobbed and weaved over the still form of my son. I tried not to stare into his empty eyes, swallowed past the terror he was dead, that he'd not be able to return to his physical form while the agitated drach souls wheeled overhead and squealed their protest of his departure. I knew exactly how they felt.

"How long." I gritted my aching jaw against the question.

"I don't know," Sass whispered. "We just found him like this. Syd, it's my fault for not watching him more closely. I'm so sorry—"

"Save it," I snapped. "For a chewing out when he gets back here." My fists settled on my hips, one foot tapping against the hardwood floor in impatience. "We both know you wouldn't have been able to stop him even if you'd caught him in the act." If he didn't return in five, four, three, two...

Gabriel suddenly gasped and sat up, color pinking his pale cheeks, leaning over to cough as the whirling ribbons shrieked their delight and wrapped around him in ecstatic hugs. I let them have their moment as my son gathered himself, looking up at last to meet my eyes with his own full of the veil still.

"We'll fight about it later," he said. Oh, would we ever. "It worked, Mom. I know where the next piece is." His grimace wasn't helping the tearing urge I had to leap on him and embrace him, to cover him in kisses and protect him from what he was doing, becoming. And what was that exactly? I had no idea. But I was afraid we were going to find out.

"Let me guess," I said with as much of my Mom in me as I could muster. "I'm not going to like it."

My son choked on a laugh, nodded. "I'm afraid not," he said. Sighed. "The heart Trill took," he said, rising to his feet to face me. "Don't ask me how she did it, but somehow she figured out how to cross the barrier." That truth settled around me as I gaped in shocked silence. Meanwhile, my son finished telling me the impossible. "I'm sorry, Mom. It's in the other Universe."

TWENTY-FOUR

This time I did lunge for him, grasping his upper arms in my hands while Sassafras gasped behind me.

I didn't shake my son. Oh, I wanted to. But the mother in me and the all-powerful Doombringer were too tightly locked in battle to allow me to do anything but hold him gently and ask the obvious question.

"You crossed over?" Dear elements, what would that mean for the Universe? Gabriel's first Gateway had opened the way for Dark Brother to come here, hadn't it? Did my son just make it possible for Creator's sibling's terrible army to cross to our Universe? I had to talk to Max, to warn him—

"No, Mom," Gabriel said as if such a suggestion was ridiculous and really I needed to take a deep breath and some heavy duty drugs to chill out already. "But I felt where Trill crossed."

The young Zornov again. Honestly, my ability to waffle back and forth between trusting her and Creator's plan and just wanting to beat some sense into her was giving me a migraine.

"Is she trying to bring the Order here?" Trust Jiao to ask the question that needed asking in a voice so much like icy resolve I actually felt better. Sassafras uncoiled from his cat body, his human form shifting through the silver Persian that still remained and into the lean, handsome young man he also was.

"I don't think so," Gabriel said, frowning a little as he rubbed at his eyes. When he met my gaze again the veil was gone, only the beloved hazel with sparks of green showing.

He still feels like spirit magic, my vampire whispered.

And Earth, Shaylee sent, equally as quiet.

So my son held all his power just as I did. Interesting.

That's all you can muster is interesting? My demon sounded offended and a little shocked.

You want me to run off on another side chase now? I prodded her with more good humor than perhaps I should have. *Really?*

She snorted and backed off. *Weenie,* she sent. *Can't handle a little divided attention, is that it?*

Sigh.

"Mom." Gabriel rubbed his hands over his upper arms as I stepped back, releasing him at last. Not a pained gesture, but as though he were suddenly cold. "I hate to tell you this, but you have to go get it."

Of course I did.

Ten minutes later, my frustrated daughter left behind under the protection of the coven in Wilding Springs, I sat on the arm of a wing backed chair in Mom's office and listened to all the people I'd gathered there to talk this out tell me all the reasons why I shouldn't cross Universes in pursuit of the heart of Creator. Why Gabriel had to be wrong, why doing so would open the way for the Order to cross over. Even as my kid met my eyes and held them with resigned determination while emotion and words swirled around us as much as the thin ribbons of the drach souls did.

I'm coming with you. He didn't sound as confident as he could have.

Keep dreaming, sweets. I stood up at last and held up my hands, winning silence. Faces turned to me, eyes watched with careful fear. Mom, Dad. Sass and Jiao. Varity with her smirk hiding most of her anxiety. Gram. I keenly missed Demetrius and, oddly, Piers. My sorcerer friend wasn't reachable, not even through the white magic I'd shared with him. I should have been worried, except I wasn't. Piers could take care of himself.

I just hoped it wasn't bad news. Void news. As in poof, there goes the Steam Union. I couldn't think like that and had no time to run off to Scotland to try to figure out what was going on with him.

My sister cleared her throat where she stood next to Mabel, Max on their other side. He stared out the window into the early evening, not speaking or offering any kind of support. That hurt me a little bit. But he had to have as much on his mind as I did.

The black ribbon on my wrist tightened when Meira spoke.

"Demonicon is down to less than two dozen planes." She didn't sound angry, just frustrated and at a loss. "We have to do something."

"We need the heart," Mabel said, her calm taking Max's accustomed place. "And if that means Syd must go to the other Universe to retrieve it, I choose to trust Creator's guidance." She nodded to my son who seemed so small and frail all of a sudden, the center of so much intense attention. But he didn't seem to mind it, taking it in stride.

"Mabel is right," he said, little voice ringing with authority. "And Mom has to go."

"Why me?" I had known for some time my son had access to information I didn't, information he'd never been able—or willing, if I was being honest about his reticence—to share. This seemed like as good a time as any to prod him.

Gabriel winced, looked away. "You just do, Mom."

I could have pulled a fast one and told him I wasn't

going unless he filled me in. But this wasn't some mother-son game we were playing, not a power struggle over him cleaning his room or doing his chores. This was life and death, the fate of the Universe. And I didn't have the right to tell the Gateway no, despite my reservations. Like I'd let anyone else run off and handle this without me.

Hey, I was a grown up. Who knew?

"You realize this is a trap." Mom's snapping anger just made me sad. "Some means Trill Zornov arranged to get you into the reach of Dark Brother and the Order."

I'd considered that. Gabriel's continuing misery didn't help much.

"So be it," I said. "We have to finish Creator's statue and in the order the pieces were meant to be returned." There was that word again, layered over Mom's reference. "What choice do we have?"

No one answered, mute frustration holding us all in a vicelike grip in the heavy air.

"I'm coming," Gabriel said, but Max chose then to turn around and face us, to speak at last.

"No," he said in his deep voice that hummed unhappily with the song of the drach. "If we are to cross, you will be our only way back." His diamond eyes met mine. "I will come with you, Sydlynn Hayle. For good or ill, let us venture into the heart of darkness together."

Tears burned my eyes at his offer. I wouldn't have had it any other way.

"Girl," Gram said, weariness in her face, in her voice, though her magic never wavered. "You are Doombringer." Like she had to remind me. "What if crossing over triggers the destruction of our Universe?"

"Our Universe, Ethpeal Hayle, is already dying." Max bowed his head to her. "Nothing Syd can do at this point will make things worse than they already are. And I have a feeling that title has a far different connotation than any of us can conceive just yet." Did he, too, know more than he was saying?

No, he sent, *I don't*. Nice of him to read my mind. *But I don't believe Creator would send you where we must go if this is all there was to who you are.*

I wasn't sure I followed his logic, but so be it.

"I would journey with you, Syd." Maybe I should have been surprised when Max's apprentice offered to come, but Jiao's offer was welcome.

"That's it," I said. "The three of us." I nodded to Mom, ready to go now. So I didn't change my mind or anything smart like that. "Just hold things together as best you can until we get back." If we came back. "This shouldn't take too long." I hoped.

"And where exactly is it you're going?" Gram's bitterness wasn't lost on me. She hated it when I left her. Well, I hated leaving her. So there. "I highly doubt Dark Brother and his pets are going to let you wander around looking for the heart."

Okay, I hadn't thought this all the way through, clearly. But Gabriel's hand was reaching for mine and I knew he had.

At least someone had.

"The only place Trill would take it, Mom," he said while sending me an image so familiar my chest ached.

Of course. It made perfect sense, as did Trill's cryptic words not so long ago. *Pay attention when Wilding Springs goes dark. Listen to your heart.* The heart of Creator waited in the Dark Universe version of home. But why there in the back yard of the house I knew so well, in a Universe I didn't?

Order, Mom, he said. *There are rules and order to this entire thing. Connections, patterns. Wilding Springs is one of them, for many reasons.* The veil was back in his eyes. *You'll know more later. For now, just trust. And go get the heart.*

I nodded, never feeling so unsure and yet confident at the same time.

I won't let you down, I sent.

His smile lit my whole world. *Oh, Mom,* he sent. *You never will.*

With a sendoff like that, how could I possibly lose?

TWENTY-FIVE

I reached for the veil then and there, not wanting to have the chance for Fate or bad luck or whatever was out there to mess with me and find a reason to keep me here. Whether a good sign or not, no giant disaster happened, not a flicker of protest from the Universe I was about to step between here and what lay beyond the barrier.

Guess that meant I was doing the right thing. Hoped that counted as a good sign.

Not here, Max sent, feeling odd in my head. What was up with him? The ribbon around my wrist flexed in agreement.

Right. I knew where he wanted to go and took us there without comment.

The backyard in Wilding Springs welcomed us, the evening air cooler, autumn rapidly approaching now as September finally turned over into October. I'd been home less than a week from my six month sojourn with the drach and it felt like forever.

Time was funny stuff. Maybe it had been forever and I just didn't know it yet.

Here. Gabriel reached for me through the veil, showed me the place where Trill had crossed. It felt squishy, soft around the crust as if she'd sealed the way behind her again but left the door open from this side. *I can make a Gateway for you once you open the veil to travel. I won't be able to leave it open, though.* He didn't sound happy about that. *Get the heart and send a message into the veil. I'll hear it and make a new Gateway for your exit.* His mind quavered, confidence shaky. So, he wasn't sure this would work.

I could either make him feel worse about it by questioning his instructions or just get on with it already. Guess which one I chose? A woman of action, yup yup.

I love you. I hugged him with my power before opening the veil, my intent to arrive in the same backyard I now occupied, only on the other side. It was hard to focus because I had no idea what I was walking into. Did it look like this one? Or was everything different? Did Wilding Springs even exist over there as it did here? An instant of panic gripped me as a Gateway sprang to life and I realized for the first time how powerful my son had become.

He was still at Harvard, wasn't he?

Be safe, Mom, Gabriel sent, softly wistful. *Come home,*

okay?

Still not completely sure. No way was I letting guilt stop either of us, though the sight of blankness on the other side of the Gateway didn't exactly raise much confidence. Didn't the other side usually appear, the destination clear, when he opened one of these things? Empty nothing wasn't the most promising of destinations. *I'll see you soon, sweets. Take care of things while we're gone.*

With that, Max on one side and Jiao on the other, I stepped into the Gate and that blank nothing.

I'd spent most of my adult life traveling the veil. I thought I knew what it felt like, as a witch, a maji, even as a drach. The living, breathing rubber membrane between planes had a distinctive feel to it, warmth that embraced me every time, its dimness no longer an issue. I always felt at home here, had only experienced confidence within the confines of the veil.

Until now. My stomach heaved as we crossed into the Gateway, the ribbon on my wrist flexing painfully in tune with my sudden loss of breath. It seemed everything flipped over on its back, shook like a wet dog then righted itself again. The very veil snarled at me, pulling and tugging at the edges of my magic, even as I slammed bodily into a barrier that felt well-known and yet like nothing I'd ever encountered before.

I didn't get a chance to ask Max what the hell was

happening—not that the drach lord would have an answer. Between one crushing heartbeat and the next I staggered unceremoniously from the irritated and disdainful embrace of the veil, spit out into my backyard.

Damn it. I spun on my heel, the same cool evening wrapping me in a breeze that smelled of autumn, the light over the screen door coming on in response to the last of the day dying in the West.

It didn't work. I reached for Gabriel to tell him we'd failed, only to catch my breath in shock.

The heart.

It was here.

Oh. My. Swearword.

"Syd," Max said with some urgency in his voice, enough I jerked around, wide-eyed, to face him. His gray skin had paled, diamond eyes sparking with anxiety. "Hurry."

No failure after all. We'd done it. We were here, in the other Universe. But this was wrong, so wrong. It looked the same, as if nothing had changed, like everything that happened back home happened here, too. How could that be when we had Creator and these people, these planes only had Dark Brother and sorcery and...

I shook myself as Jiao pinched my arm sharply on one side while the black ribbon growled on my right wrist.

Right. Focus, Syd.

It was easy enough to find the heart, the pulsing of it familiar if only because of my connection to the Stronghold. Did Gabriel give me the ability to find it? Or did it reach for me because it knew me? No matter the reason, my magic reached back to its demands and, a moment later, a small, red shape popped out of the ground from under a flagstone next to the back door and hurtled toward me. I cupped the plastic heart in my palm, turning it over in shock.

It couldn't be. But it had to be.

Max nodded, looking around, hands flexing at his sides. "We have to go." He sounded like he didn't believe it could be this easy.

I had to agree. But here we were, heart in hand. I reached for the veil, for Gabriel. Even as the back door opened and Ameline stepped out into the fall night.

I gaped at her, taking a second to realize she was gaping in return. What was she doing here? My mind blanked as the door opened wider and Quaid appeared behind her. Put his hand on her shoulder, another at her waist.

Like they were together.

"I killed you." Her hushed voice cut through the night air. Max's power prodded me but I was lost to this.

"You first, sister." I drove my hands into my pockets, hiding the heart from her view. Her eyes widened further, if that was possible.

"You're her." She shuddered, looked over her shoulder at Quaid. "Doombringer."

He didn't take his eyes off me, glaring in that way I knew so well. And didn't.

Surreal.

I felt Max and Jiao reaching for the veil, let them do my job for me while I stood there, staring at the reality that happened here.

"You killed me?" Stupid question, she'd said so, didn't she?

"I did." Ameline shrugged off Quaid's hands, took a step closer. "You deserved it." Sounded like she thought she needed to repeat her performance. "And you killed me?"

"I hate to tell you what a bitch you were, but…" Was I having fun? No, impossible. Syd, get a grip already. Life and death, remember?

A tiny smile twitched her lip, curiosity in her face. She looked more like the Ameline I came to like, the one in the maji chamber back home. And nothing like the young woman raised by the Dumonts.

"I was about to say the same about you." She hesitated. "You seem different." Was she doubting herself?

"I've met both sides of you," I said. "So I'm not so surprised you turned out different here." But who had I been in her Universe? "I take it you weren't raised

Dumont?"

She shuddered, backed away again, Quaid's hands protecting her. They both wore rings, a normal sentiment my ex-husband and I never really took seriously.

Married? No way.

"I'm a Hayle sorcerer," she said.

And therein lay the utter truth of everything. This wasn't my Universe, some flipped version of it. There was only sorcery here, no witches and vampires and other races I was used to. No broken magicks. And no me, not anymore.

Ameline was a Hayle. I didn't think I'd ever learn to accept that.

Syd, we must go. Max felt desperate. Where was the Gateway? I searched through the veil for the pocket door Trill left.

And found nothing.

Oops.

Ameline spoke again, distraction I didn't need. "Why are you destroying our Universe?" She sounded honestly upset, frustrated. Quaid hugged her, glared at me.

"We know who you are, Doombringer," he said. "Are you here to try to end everything now?"

Wait, they were blaming me? "You have no idea what's really going on," I said. Hesitated. I didn't have time to explain and did it really matter if they believed me or not? Besides, they were kind of right. By reassembling

Creator's statue, wasn't I bringing about all our doom?

Was this what Doombringer truly meant?

Before I could push words out of my gaping mouth, Ameline shook her head, looked away.

"It doesn't matter now," she said. I had an instant, one in which the ribbon on my wrist flexed in fury before the air around us rushed outward, cutting off my oxygen for a brief moment.

The next, the backyard was filled with towering bodies in shining armor, all their power focused on me.

TWENTY-SIX

She called them. Of course she did. As the Order closed in and trapped us, I shook myself free of the curiosity I had for this Ameline, for Quaid and the two dark haired girls poking their noses out the back door. One looked familiar, the youngest having enough of Ethie in her I realized the truth. No Gabriel. Of course, no Gabriel.

He, at least, was one of a kind.

The idea made me want to laugh in the face of the crushing power of the soldiers around me. Ameline and Quaid seemed small in comparison, the backyard space shrunk to a tiny patch of grass trampled under shining metal boots. The full weight of their energy settled on my shoulders, driving me to my knees. Irresistible their power, an equal to mine. Sure, I might have been able to take on one, maybe two. But twenty?

We were so screwed. And it was all my fault for letting myself get distracted.

"Hayle family." One of the soldiers, his armor more decorative than the others, stomped forward, his magic crushing me as though he enjoyed the experience. The black ribbon twitched and the pressure lessened, to the grunting surprise of the soldier. He ignored me then, focusing through the tiny slit in his visor on Ameline and Quaid. Neither looked all that eager to be the center of his attention. "Your aid is greatly appreciated and will be brought to the attention of our Master."

"No need," Ameline said in a voice that shook. "We are honored to serve."

Yeah, right. Sounded like it. Never mind I should have been trembling in fear, shouldn't I? Shaking in my boots, ready to curl up in a ball and call it quits. This was the Order. They'd scared the bejeebuz pants off me the last time I'd seen them, their giant army marching toward the Gateway that Gabriel made in the Stronghold's underchamber.

So why then was I on the verge of irritated frustration when the leader turned to me? Defiance and rage mixed together while the girls thumbed their noses—and some rude gestures—his way.

"If you're about done," I said at my most sarcastic.

He stopped, shock clear in the power rippling around me. So, wasn't used to being spoken to like that, huh?

Syd, Max's voice made it to me, strained and tight with worry. *What are you doing?*

You should know my temper by now. I flexed my magic, pushing myself to my feet by sheer force of will. The lead soldier pushed back but damn it I was pissed and the girls were too. And the black ribbon? Well, it had enough, thanks. I caught the shock in Ameline's face, the way that shock turned to speculation when I carefully crossed my arms over my chest and glared back at him.

"Nice suit," I said. "Must ring like a bastard when someone hits you."

"No one has ever made contact." He sounded proud of that fact.

With the final ounce of power I had, I tapped him between the eyes, making his helmet sing.

Syd. Dear elements, Syd. What was I thinking? A choking giggle rose in the back of my throat as the leader took a surprised step back, shaking his head.

I was toast. But I'd be damned if I wasn't going down without a snark.

Maybe I would have made further inroads, but there was only so much I could do considering the press of power around me. And, when two young men and three women pushed past the soldiers to observe me, I realized I'd placed my fear in the wrong race.

I knew them, what they were. It was easy to see the alternate shapes of them, so accustomed I was to Max, to

Jiao and Sass. Only these weren't drach or *lóng* or magicked demon boys trapped in the bodies of cats.

Dragons. There be dragons here.

The two men looked like medieval versions I'd see on the covers of old fantasy novels. One of the women was clearly a water type with pale skin and hair and a hint of the ocean around her. But it was the last two that shook me the most.

I was wrong about the *lóng* not being present. These were the evolution of the drach, those we'd thought dead, near extinction. Were they then able to evolve here and not die out as they had at home?

Wait, no. Not so, not when traces of elemental power clung to them, not when they felt exactly like Jiao and even a bit like me.

I was so floored by this revelation, I held still as the lead man and woman approached, ignoring me in favor of Jiao. My fighting heart stilled.

Daughter. Their minds combined to speak to her, their twining, Chinese dragon bodies clear to me as they addressed my friend.

Jiao, normally more stone like than Creator's statue itself gaped at them with eyes wide like a child.

The battle went out of me, the ability to fight back. The world flashed as the lead soldier saluted the staring pair of Ameline and Quaid, the veil engulfing us. But not the veil I knew. The darkness I'd gone looking for in my alternate backyard might not have been visible there, but it was here, embedded in the membrane between planes. At least, what was left of it.

They were in the exact same boat we were. Good to have that confirmed.

I tried to reach for Max but had been cut off. And while I knew I could get to him if I used my white sorcery, I held back. They'd find out about Creator's ultimate power evolution soon enough. Until then, I'd like to keep it safe in my back pocket—with Creator's disguised heart—for as long as I could.

Not that escape was going to be possible. I knew it the second we exited the veil and entered a giant, arching chamber, the ceiling covered in rocky outgrowths, the floor crusted with more, all filled to the brim with dragons.

I'd thought before we were screwed. I had no idea what that term actually meant until all the creatures roared at our meeting.

I was a strong person, have always held my own when it came to being hurt, whether as a girl on the soccer field winning with a torn shin or a bloody nose or facing down creatures with magic and fire. But I'd never felt pain like I did in that moment, and screamed in response. I just couldn't hold it in.

They didn't die out, the *lóng*. The evolution of the drach simply came here. By choice. And there was nothing I could do to stand against them. The Order weren't the ones I should fear.

I shook my head, dazed by agony, spotting in the fog of pain a handful of drach scattered in human form among the *lóng*. Shoulders curved, heads down, they seemed subservient to the *lóng*. And, for all I knew, they were. Made sense, didn't it, even to my stunned mind.

No help there, then.

From the horrified look on Max's face, the rapture on Jiao's, I knew we were lost and that whatever had driven Trill to betray me for the last time I would never, ever forgive her.

But it wasn't until one of the drach turned, bowed to the *lóng*, I understood Max's true despair. The form of its towering dragon body seemed misshapen, damaged. And as it spun and left the cavern, I understood why.

Someone had cut off his wings.

I didn't have time to mourn the loss, to register the hideousness of the act. We were herded with magic out of the cavern, down a long, sloping corridor three stories in height, the ceiling towering overhead as *lóng* shifted shape and wheeled above us. I staggered as I went, overwhelmed by everything I'd seen so far, but the pressure of the *lóng*'s continuing control kept me moving.

Huge doors swung open at the end of the corridor, the room beyond full of ranks upon ranks of the Order's soldiers, each of them standing at perfect attention. This was some kind of underground parade, had to be, bigger than two football fields end to end, reminding me in many ways of the forced pomp and showmanship of the demon plane. Wait a minute. I knew the rock of this place, recognized the black stone. But no demons lived here, did they? Demons didn't exist here.

Ostrogotho. The Seat on Demonicon. That same place housed the Order.

Of course it did.

The biggest soldier in the bunch strode forward while I swallowed that prideful thought, almost a foot taller than his soldiers, towering at an impressive seven and a half feet. But, when he pulled free his looming helmet, I realized my mistake. Maybe seven feet minus the headdress. Which made me wonder if his boots were lifts.

Yeah, even now I reached for humor to keep me from melting down.

He blustered and yelled at us for about five minutes, pale cheeks pinking, thinning blond hair showing a pulsing vein in his scalp. His soldiers watched his tirade in utter silence. I caught, "Commander Treeger," and "death to Doombringer," and a couple of other random words, but that was about it while he did his best to impress me or something. He was so loud and the room so echoing it just wasn't possible to make him out.

But when he fell silent it was clear his soldiers did. To a soul they shouted, "Oogha!" or something like it and clamped their right fists to their left shoulders in salute.

I'd be more intimidated if I wasn't pissed off all over again.

"Whatever," I said in the sudden silence as the echo of their fealty died out.

He gaped, pale blue eyes bulging. I liked that look on him, at least until he slammed magic into me. I was ready for him though, pulling out the white sorcery and, on impulse, tying it through the black ribbon on my wrist. Together we pushed back.

It was like shoving against a mountain, an immovable and impossibly high peak that had stood for millennia without shaking its foundations. Fear I'd bitten off more than I could chew this time died when I snapped it in half and tossed it aside with help from the girls.

We're dead anyway, my demon snarled. *Might as well go down showing them messing with Doombringer is the wrong thing to do.*

Hell, yeah, Shaylee sent, sounding more like her fiery sister in that moment than her usual self.

Agreed, my vampire snarled in full spirit power mode. *Crush him, ladies.*

While her order was a bit out of our reach, my heart leaped when I felt him move. Just a fraction, the barest bit of flex, but it was there. I think we confused him, the myriad of minds and powers. Surely he had no idea what white sorcery was, or elemental magic. And with every push from the girls, from the ribbon and my own personal power, he swayed.

When he finally took a single step back, I formed a wall between us and nodded once.

"That all you got?"

My demon laughed like a maniac in my head.

"Doombringer." He said the name like he feared me. I'd take that, thanks.

Before he could hit me again or whatever it was he planned, Jiao stepped forward and put her hand on my shoulder. I turned to her, hoping she had something in mind. Maybe with Max's help we could bully and bluff our way out of this.

Syd, she sent. *I'm sorry.*

And everything went black.

TWENTY-SEVEN

I woke up alone. Groaned as I rolled over on my side, my whole body hurting, taking a moment to realize what had actually happened.

That Jiao, my friend, had betrayed me to the Order.

No, there had to be a reason, an explanation. I sat up on the stone bench where I'd been lying, passed out for who knew how long. A quick inventory of my person turned up no physical injuries aside from feeling like I'd run headlong into a brick wall. The black ribbon remained with me, tight around my wrist, though it had fallen silent and I wondered if it had done so to protect itself. Likely. If it was from this Universe as Max and I both suspected, there might be those who would recognize the drach soul for what it was and try to take it from me.

Feeling oddly possessive, I ran one hand over it before moving on.

Demon? I almost hesitated to ask.

Here. She grumbled something about traitors and fire and death but I didn't bother to ask her to elaborate.

Shaylee? Again the affirmative.

We're all here, Syd. My vampire stretched inside me. *Though we were all knocked out by that blow.*

I wondered then if Jiao had been hurt. *Don't we have some kind of defense mechanism against that?*

We do. My demon's grim joy felt like glass shards on my insides. *I believe that disgusting little Black Soul sorcerer almost died because of it when he attacked us in Hong Kong.* Smug much?

Well, there was hope we'd done the *lóng* some damage.

Max? I reached out for him, my power—our power—hitting a wall. And not like the mountain the Order's leader had been. This was a slippery, slimy shell I couldn't even find a spot to push against. It slithered out of the way but formed into rigid immobility if I tried to shove my way through. Tired and burned out for the moment, I retreated from it, pushing myself to a standing position.

The room was large enough, carved out of the black stone of the place. More and more I was sure this was the plane I knew as Ostrogotho.

Agreed, my demon sent.

Not that it will help us, my vampire sent. *Any advantage we might have knowing where we are is gone considering this place is nothing like the Ostrogotho we know.*

Well, there was that. *Way to pop the bubble of optimism*, my demon snarked.

You're better off focusing on reality than fantasy, my friend, my vampire sent.

I cut off their impending fight with a sharp intake of breath. My hands had slid into my pockets, fingers on the right sliding over something smooth and small.

"No way," I breathed, fishing out the red plastic heart. "How did they miss it?" And why hadn't Jiao told them about it?

My demon chortled her glee. *Who cares how or what that traitor was thinking? We still have it. That has to count for something.*

I was willing to accept that more than my vampire's need for reality.

Gabriel. Shaylee's soft voice shook with hope. *Maybe we can use it to reach him.*

I didn't wait or second guess myself. I tried. And hit the same gross, sludgy wall.

Even my vampire seemed vexed when I finally gave up and glared at the only exit, a heavy metal door with a small, barred window hole at the top.

So much for that idea. Shaylee shivered. *Sorry.*

Don't be, I sent. *I'm not leaving here without Max anyway.*

And the traitorous Jiao, my demon sent. *I'll drag her long ass kicking and screaming all the way home just to see the look on her face when I show her how much we disapprove of her actions.*

Usually my demon's bluster made me sigh. In this moment, I embraced it, if only to feel powerful for a second.

Why didn't they take the heart? My vampire's musing was the last thing I wanted to think about. I paced the stone floor, prodding the shields at odd intervals in an attempt to test their strength. Nothing changed. Naturally.

Maybe Creator protected it from them finding it? That could have happened, though my demon sounded like she didn't believe it, either.

Or, more likely, Shaylee sent, *whatever Trill did to disguise it is hiding it.*

That did make sense. *But surely, if she betrayed us*—and she had, hadn't she?—*Jiao would have told them about it.*

Not one of the girls had an answer for that. So I switched lines of thought. *Why did Trill send us here?* I hated the faint wail in my mental voice as I jerked myself to a halt, resisting the urge to pinch myself to pull my pounding heart under control. It was hard not to feel like a rat in a trap, to fall into helplessness.

No way. Not doing it.

There has to be a purpose. The reasonable tone in my vampire's voice calmed me. I held onto her as she went on. *While you might doubt her, I have had my ideas about Trillia Zornov from the beginning. I don't think she's betrayed us, only done what Creator intended.*

Fate, damn it. I'd run headlong into it so many times I was about ready to toss everything and become a hermit.

Whatever the reason, my vampire sent, *we must stand fast against what comes next.*

I didn't like the fear in her voice or the answering terror in my heart.

What do you mean? My demon sounded wary but as if she didn't get it. Not like we did.

Dark Brother. Shaylee whispered the name and my demon flinched.

You think he's actually here? I'd never heard her voice squeak before.

We can handle anything, my vampire sent.

A god? Shaylee sighed. *I think you overestimate us.*

I clutched at the heart in my hand, returned it to my pocket. *If he finds it, we lose everything.*

Then, that secret we focus on, my vampire sent. *Everything else he comes for, he can take. But that is ours to keep.*

Easier said than done. But it was something to hold onto. And, a moment later as the darkness in my cell increased, the pressure of something massive approaching driving the breath from my body and making my knees collapse under me, I wondered if we had the strength for even that.

Dark Brother was coming. No. He was here.

I'd feared him since Gabriel opened the first Gateway, since seeing his black form, flames for eyes and mouth, felt the devouring hunger of his presence. There were times I'd been woken by nightmares of that experience, driven to the brink of sobbing in my sleep from terror.

And he'd still been on the other side.

This was far different. More intimate. And, as Dark Brother's weight settled around me and devoured me, I felt no pride, no shame when I screamed my sanity away.

TWENTY-EIGHT

I don't know what I expected. A voice, maybe, a personality? I encountered nothing of the sort when Dark Brother swarmed over me and swallowed me whole. Laid me bare in an instant to the core of my spirit, dug deep into everything that made me who I was and tore it loose to examine closely while I could do nothing.

Nothing.

Power like I'd never felt engulfed me and ate me alive while I screamed and screamed without a single sound emerging from that thick, impenetrable blackness.

I couldn't even be afraid. All emotion, every thought, down to the barest bits and pieces of my makeup was taken and shaken and discarded as Creator's sibling used me up for what I knew and threw me away.

And I'd thought to conceal anything from that

presence? Considered myself strong enough to hide even the basest of secrets? I had no idea. No. Idea.

He finally left me, a puddle of nothing that I recognized of myself on the floor of my cell. The stone under my numb cheek had become soaked with tears and saliva from my gaping mouth. Battered and bruised within, aching from the blackness of his assault, I could do nothing but stare into the emptiness of the quiet prison and block it all out.

It was the soft, insistent nudging at my right hand that finally broke me free of my paralysis, drawing my attention where I thought curiosity dead. My chin tipped, my gaze traveling down to my hip. I was on my side, partially turned over, right hand a limp and lifeless thing that felt detached from my body. When my fingers twitched it had nothing to do with my actions. No, it was the quivering, shimmering lump of black bouncing like it was alive in my palm that triggered a visceral response.

My fingers closed over the smooth, warm ribbon of darkness that normally clung to my wrist. And, when they fell open again, it slithered loose of its tight, tense orb shape, sliding yet again around my flesh and squeezing tight.

Leaving the small, pulsing thing it had protected against my skin.

Plastic heart, dented on one side, a broken clasp at the top where once maybe it had hooked to a keychain or a necklace. At least, that's how it appeared. I knew better. And the moment I registered the piece of Creator was safe, it began to glow.

With a gentleness that was the only antidote to the cruel destruction of Dark Brother, Creator's kind heart reached within me and began the healing process.

Again, I had no idea what real power felt like, not until this day when first the evil of one side tore me to pieces leaving the goodness of the other to put me back together again. I have no idea how long it took for Creator's heart to undo enough I could sit up. I wiped at the moisture on my face with disgust and loathing, resting my forehead on my bent knees. Sobs escaped, at last, crushing, devouring things that needed to emerge so I could come the rest of the way back.

I wasn't alone in the gentle ministrations of the power of the heart. The girls returned to me, slowly and with great hurt, embracing me when they were able to accept what had been done to us. I never missed them so much as I did when they came back to me this time. Nothing like losing them to quiet sleep when I'd been drach. Far worse than even when my demon left me on purpose. Their pain and suffering was my pain and suffering, multiplied by three.

I think I slept then, sitting up with my arms around my knees, the warmth of Creator passing through me and into the girls inside my head. All I know is when I opened my eyes again, I felt more myself than I had a right to after what we'd endured.

Anger woke with me. My favorite.

We won't survive that again. My vampire's quiet acceptance was shared by all of us. I clenched my hand around the heart of Creator and pulled myself to my feet, body aching from the awkward position we'd been in, head throbbing and soul full of fury.

I know, I sent. *Time to get the hell out of here.*

Big talk, considering. But I couldn't contemplate even for a second another encounter with Dark Brother. The very thought made me want to fall to my knees and scream all over again. Carefully, with the help of the trio of personalities in my mind, I walled off all memory of his presence, of the assault. We'd deal with it later.

Maybe.

I did a quick check of my power, found we were none the worse for wear physically and energetically at least. The mental and emotional abuse... well. Walls of denial were made for this kind of thing.

Oddly, my white sorcery seemed the least affected, humming softly in response when I reached for it. As though Dark Brother's attack hadn't touched it.

Could it be possible? Shaylee sounded shaken.

Creator's ultimate magic never reached this Universe if what we know is true, my vampire sent.

Well, the cat's out of the bag now, my demon snarled.

Maybe, I sent. *Maybe not. After all, Belaisle must have known about it, thanks to Jean Marc. So I doubt it's a huge secret. But it might be something Dark Brother has chosen to ignore if he doesn't understand it.* Like he had anything to fear. Or thought he did. Arrogance could work in our favor. I rubbed at the black ribbon around my wrist, sent it thanks for protecting the heart. Because I'd failed utterly.

Its answering power embrace gave me a bit of hope, at least. And triggered a flash of recognition. I knew this soul, was far more open to it in this moment than I'd been all along, thanks to Dark Brother. But who was it? There was enough of a difference its identity eluded me. But I did know it, of that I was certain.

Who then in this Universe—which of the drach—was it?

I paced the four walls of the stone cell, once large enough it seemed, now tiny to my desperate need to escape. Any and all attempts to reach Gabriel were blocked by the slithering, slimy shielding. I was just throwing my energy away. Finally, anger at a peak, ready to try smashing my way out despite knowing it was a lost cause, I paused in the center of the room and clenched myself against the truth.

Trapped. I was trapped. And there was absolutely no way out. I'd never in my life felt so helpless. There was always something, a way to be made, a chance of escape or an opportunity to fight back. But right here, right now, nothing.

I looked down at the heart in my hand. Could I access the power of Creator to beat my way out? The moment my mind latched onto that possibility the faint warmth of the piece died and the heart went silent.

I tried not to think of it as a traitor, considering it had saved me. And wondered then where the voice of it was, the personality that seemed to live inside each piece. Wished it would talk to me, even if it was as frustrating and irritating as some of the other pieces had been.

Silence. And hopelessness.

There is a reason we are here. We all focused on my vampire when she spoke. Clung to her words as a unit when she went on. *Fate has led us to this place. And it's time we trusted Creator's plan.*

Could I toss my own fears and doubts and just trust?

Do you have a choice? My vampire's soft whisper was for me alone.

So hard, giving up my free will for the faith she suggested. Impossible, maybe. The woman I'd become had been created in fire and strife, taught to think for herself, to act and believe in her own power and the strength of her will. And here I was, that woman, trying to step back from everything I'd learned. Everything I'd been taught by time and Fate and battle, and just abandon it for belief this was the way things were supposed to happen.

I know, my vampire sighed. *And yet?*

And yet.

Creator had a plan for me. I was Doombringer. For good or ill, like it or not, I was here, now, in this place, at this time, with no hope and no prospects, the heart of the Universe in my hands. Letting go felt like quitting.

Until I did it, in a rush of need so powerful I gasped. Covered my face in my hands, the hard plastic heart pressed to my lips. And felt Her pulse against my cold skin in a hug of magic.

When I dropped my hands, looked down, I saw at last the stone shape of the real heart outlined faintly in my grasp, though the piece itself remained in its disguised form. And nodded to it. No. To Her.

You won't let me die here, I sent to Her.

No, She answered, faint, distant.

Okay then. Faith it was.

I actually felt better, hopeful, calm. Funny, nothing had really changed about my situation. And everything had.

Even more so when the door to my cell clanged, the lock turning, and the way opened. I looked up, feeling the most at peace I had since I was drach, and stared down the tall, armor clad figure who entered my prison, power radiating from him like a shroud of darkness.

The Order had come for me.

I was ready.

TWENTY-NINE

No attack came, no demands or even conversation. The soldier of the Order simply stood there, observing me through the slits in his shining helmet, tall, wide shouldered body rigid and observant.

I glared back, beginning to feel like a rat in a glass box, hating the trapped knot of anxiety in my stomach. I'd embraced the peace Creator's heart offered but old habits die hard. It was far easier to return to the familiar anger I used as my shield for so long. Finally, when so much time passed my discomfort no longer allowed me to stay silent, I crossed my arms over my chest and tossed my head.

"Well?" My voice crackled, snapping with fury and frustration. "What are you waiting for?" I was so ready for the impending fight. He didn't stand a chance.

Yeah, keep telling yourself that, Hayle. And maybe

you'd survive another ten seconds.

A sound emerged from behind his helmet, so unexpected I felt my face crumple in shock, all the anger running out of me a moment, only to surge back when I realized the bastard was laughing.

He was laughing. At me.

Oh, no he did *not*.

"You won't find my foot up your ass very damned funny," I snarled.

His gauntleted hands reached up, removed his helmet. I clenched my jaw against what might be underneath, though I knew the Order soldiers were as human appearing as I was. I wasn't expecting to find him attractive. Pale gray eyes and dirty blond hair, the way his jaw darkened from his need to shave or the fact there was something achingly and instantly recognizable about him I couldn't put my finger on.

No. I didn't know him. It was my need to find a way to escape driving me to connect with him so I could get the hell out of here. That was all.

Even the girls seemed doubtful about my logic, but all of us let it go as he spoke.

"I'm shocked by such unladylike threats," he said in a deep, expressive voice, full, wide lips turning up on one side in a smile. Laughter lurked in his gaze, in the set of his shoulders as he tucked his helmet under one arm. "You kiss your mother with that mouth?"

Splutter. What the hell was this? Torture by snark?

He looked me up and down, raking me purposely with his gaze. When he met my eyes again, one of his arching eyebrows lifted, still with humor on his handsome face. "You're the Doombringer?"

My jaw jumped. Arrogant asshat. I can't say why I was so offended by his casual and jovial attitude. Except this was serious business, wasn't it? His damned god just stripped me bare and left me for mush. His people wanted me dead, had captured and imprisoned me, were trying to break into my Universe and take over. And this was funny to him?

"So they tell me." I pulled myself to my full height, knowing my reach was no match for his well over six feet. And took stock of myself with grim embarrassment I crushed with anger. Okay, so maybe I didn't look all that impressive at the moment. Not with my white t-shirt filthy and torn, my jeans about the same shape, the laces of one sneaker dangling dangerously around my ripped tread. I blew absently at a stray lock of hair that had escaped what remained of my ponytail and did my best to look impressive anyway.

He smirked.

Of anything he could have done at that moment, smirking was the wrong choice. I snarled under my breath and let some power out.

"I'm in stealth mode," I said.

He laughed out loud at that, a ringing sound, rich and vibrant. It offended me to the core of my being. I have no idea how I refrained from crossing the distance between us and punching him in the face, but I did. Good for me.

He finally stopped, genuine humor fading at last, though his smile never left him. And, in that instant, he delivered another massive shock as he stepped aside, clearing the exit, one arm extended as he freed his helmet with the other and gestured for me to precede him.

"Are you going to stand there all day?" The metal sang like a struck bell as he lifted the helm to face height and paused, grinning. "Or are you going to come with me?"

"Why should I?" My question stopped his hands, the helmet part way over his face. When he finally lowered it the rest of the way, his good humor came through in the hollow echo of his voice.

"I thought you wanted to save the Universe, Sydlynn Hayle." He paused, waited, expectant.

A trap, a trick. My demon's power swirled in acute agitation.

Possibly, Shaylee sent, troubled herself but more trusting than any of us, it felt like.

Softening us up, my demon sent. *We should stay put.*

And do what, exactly? My vampire sighed. *Let's find out what he wants. It's not as though we have much choice anyway, do we?*

She was right. *He could force us to go.*

He could try. My demon was going to be a problem, clearly.

Trust. Faith. Belief. It was all or nothing, wasn't it? And from the way he stood there, quiet and non-confrontational, I had to choose to do as Creator asked me and just take that leap of hell yeah.

If this is some tactic of theirs, we'll be ready. As ready as we could be, under the circumstances. That assurance seemed to make my demon settle at least. But confusion and the need to trust wasn't a happy mix while I stepped forward, the fight going out of me briefly as I grasped firmly onto Fate and Creator's heart, the black ribbon tight around my wrist.

And took a chance this was what was intended all along.

THIRTY

It felt odd to walk, unfettered and with only the single Order soldier striding along beside me as I took the obvious route down the corridor outside my cell and to the deep, narrow staircase at the far end. There were only a few doors along the path. This must have been where they kept their most dangerous prisoners.

Keep telling yourself that, my demon half-laughed through her continuing irritation. At least she'd found her sense of humor again.

My guard closed the distance between us part way to the top, one gauntleted hand grasping my elbow. I could have fought off his touch but chose to just observe and have faith, a massive leap for me.

Proud of you, my vampire muttered.

Me too, actually.

Part of me shuddered deep inside as we emerged at

the top of the staircase into a large room. Rows of all kinds of metal implements hung from the walls, chains dangling from the ceilings. Torture chamber? Could they be more archaic? And yet it was hard not to react, to have a gut instinct of terror as I brushed past one of the hulking mechanisms. Dried blood flaked to the floor, into a wet pool of something dark and sticky.

My companion didn't seem concerned by the sight, merely leading me out through a doorway and into a corridor on the other side. Polished black stone I knew well helped settle my stomach and my mind. If I could pretend I was on Demonicon, in the Seat in Ostrogotho, maybe I could control the spinning need my brain had to panic and run away screaming from what was coming.

Since I had no idea actually what that was, I'd do my best to keep it together until shrieking like a banshee and fleeing for my life became necessary.

I felt them before we encountered them, a marching column of Order soldiers meeting and passing us without a word. Not even a grunt or a nod to my guard, the dozen or so armor clad figures trotting past with perfect precision. Made me wrinkle my nose in judgment of their obedience.

Best I could do under the circumstances.

But it was our brief encounter with three *lóng* that made me the most afraid. The leader, a tall woman with a braid of blonde hair that swung to the floor—reminding me of Mabel's black plaits, though this was no drach—ran her gaze over me on the way by, but she ignored us, her companions talking quietly and not even bothering to look up. Their magic lingered a little and I again felt traces of demon and other magicks.

I took that as further confirmation the *lóng* had come from my Universe. Through what method, what channel I had no idea. But Max and I had thought the *lóng* near extinction. Instead, it turned out, they'd come here, hadn't they? He'd said they'd begun to vanish centuries ago. There were times Max wasn't quite accurate in his timelines. Was there an event I didn't know about, some disaster that could mark the crossing of the *lóng* to this Universe?

Didn't matter, I guess. Except that they didn't belong here. And having them might have tipped things into Dark Brother's corner.

Either they have no idea who we are, Shaylee sent, clearly not following my line of thought as she exhaled a sigh of relief, *or our guide has chops*.

I hadn't thought that far ahead. Who was he, anyway? And where the hell were we going?

So weird to be in this place, feeling powerless. It had been a very long time since I was the lightweight in the room, if ever. But striding the halls of the Order's base in the Dark Universe, I knew real helplessness. Gone was my ability to just use power to control and protect.

Everyone we encountered—including the soldier at my side—had as much magic as I did, if not more. That was sobering and knocked the wind continually out of my attempt at raising sail against my own shrinking ego.

Way to make a girl feel like she didn't matter even a little bit.

When we finally stopped beside a tall, narrow door of black metal, I resisted pulling my arm free out of spite and let him open the way with power. He shoved me with gentle insistence through the gap. The fact he was being respectful and not acting like I was an enemy held my temper in check.

For now.

The smallish room on the other side really wasn't. It was twice the size of Mom's office at Harvard, dominated by a large, high table and giant wooden chairs with elaborate carvings all over their tall backs. But it felt small compared to the giant woman who stood at the far end, her fists resting on the shining table surface, her own braid flame red, green eyes sparking with anger.

No, not anger. Frustration and worry. I knew that look as I approached her and she straightened. I'd seen it often enough in the mirror to know she tried to hide her concern behind a façade. Now I really was curious, despite myself.

Hope, my vampire whispered.

Indeed.

"Commander." My guide swept his helmet free again, bowing at the waist to her. "The prisoner, as requested."

She waved him off, her shoulders as broad as his, her face pinched, lips tight. She'd have been attractive in an Amazonian kind of way if she didn't look so stressed. In fact, she reminded me of Chambrelle Strait, Sunny's human servant. Which made me think of the vampires, and the void, and Dark Brother.

Bad train of trouble, there. The light at the end was definitely an oncoming disaster.

Movement turned my head, caught in my peripheral vision and I gasped softly before I could stop myself. Mabel stepped from the shadows, came to stand next to the woman my guard named Commander. But this wasn't my Mabel with her steadfast gaze and powerful presence. I saw her drach shape around her, felt keenly the loss of the bulk of her wings behind her. I sensed the ache of longing and endless agony of their removal, trying not to focus on the charred stumps behind her shoulders. This drach's long hair was gone, shorn close to her scalp, her handsome face leaned out compared to my Mabel, deeply lined and more scaled as her drach form came through further. Only her diamond eyes seemed the same, bottomless and without judgment.

"You know her." It wasn't a question. Commander's voice was deep, resonant.

I shrugged. "I know someone like her."

The soldier who'd brought me here shifted beside me as if he wanted to speak but remained quiet. What was this? I glanced at him before fixing his boss with a dark look.

She was looking me up and down, almost disappointed. "You're certain she's Doombringer?"

The Order soldier at my side laughed, the same kind, authentic sound that pissed me off all over again. "She's in stealth mode," he said. And winked at me.

Now, normally under circumstances like these I might have held my tongue or even been amused by his casual toss of my own excuse for my lack of present polish. Okay, who am I kidding? Temper, temper, Syd.

I'd felt so powerless to this point I just couldn't take it anymore. With a dull roar that grew in strength and volume, I shoved aside all worry and took on the full mantle of the magic I held inside me. Fed by my demon, by Shaylee, my vampire and so much more, I pressed myself upward and outward, taking on the physical form of all three of my personas, combining them until I towered, shoulders pressed to the immensely tall ceiling, amber eyes glowing into my peripheral vision, white skin on fire, green tinted hair waving around me as my drach heritage sprouted wings across my back.

"IS THIS BETTER?" My voice boomed through the room, bouncing from the walls, the floor, hitting the watchers with power and volume so violent they all wavered.

Instead of being afraid, the Commander sighed and nodded. Her lack of concern kind of ruined the moment and I found myself shrinking again, feeling a bit like a child caught doing something she shouldn't. At least my captors didn't seem concerned by my show of pique. Only then did I quiver at the thought such a display could have attracted unwanted attention. Rather than appearing worried, the big woman sank into a seat and sat back.

I did the same without being asked, no longer caring I looked like crap. Who was I trying to impress, anyway? I was who I was. And for the first time since I'd been captured, I felt like maybe, just maybe, things weren't as dark as they seemed.

"Oliver, sit. You're part of this, whether I like it or not." She waved at the soldier behind me. He grinned before taking his own place at the table, though Mabel chose to remain standing.

He laughed then, leaning in to tap me on the shoulder. "You weren't kidding about stealth mode," he said.

Sigh.

His commander scowled at him. "I am Shonya Opal," she said. Hesitated like there was a further identifier to add, then dropped it. "Secondary Commander of the First Line of the Order."

Whatever the hell that meant. "Nice to meet you."

Wow, polite, Syd? Seemed appropriate.

Your mother would be proud, Shaylee sent.

It seemed to satisfy the commander who nodded, though her anxiety seemed worse than ever. "You have caused us no end of trouble, Doombringer."

I shrugged. "Yeah, that sounds familiar," I said.

A chuckle from Oliver. Okay, maybe I wasn't so annoyed with him anymore.

Shonya exhaled heavily, shaking her head. Her thick red braid coiled in her lap, hissing as if it were alive when she moved. "I hope you understand and value the risk we take bringing you here like this."

"Maybe if I knew what the hell was going on," I said at my most calm.

Her eyes flashed to Oliver and she grimaced. "I take it my envoy told you nothing of our people or this meeting." Not a question. She seemed like someone who didn't ask many, instead used to telling instead of requesting.

It would serve him right, the smartass, to get him in trouble. Instead I shrugged. "I have no idea," I said. "Though I can assume this attempt at subterfuge means you're not under Dark Brother's watchful eye 24/7." She seemed confused at the reference but answered.

"If you mean our Master," she said, "he is all knowing, all seeing." But she sounded like she was repeating something taught as a child, a rote saying.

I doubt that's true, my vampire sent. *If so, such a meeting should be impossible, yes?*

"For an all knowing, all seeing king of everything, he's falling down on the job." Felt good to bluster, even a bit. "Or maybe he doesn't care you're plotting against him." I glanced around at the three of them, taking in their mutual discomfort, the fact Shonya looked up at the ceiling as if expecting death to crash down on us. The fact it didn't happen gave me courage to go on. "You are plotting against him, I take it?" Oliver shifted next to me, a bit wild around the eyes, smirking as if this wasn't funny but he couldn't help himself. Made him seem more human, more vulnerable, less scary Order dude I had to hate. And shifted my thinking instantly from self-protect mode to maybe this might work out after all. "Fill me in, please, Commander Opal. I'm listening."

The big woman leaned forward, hands twice the size of mine resting on the table, clasped in front of her. I'd say one thing for the Order, they didn't go half way in size. Reminded me once again of Demonicon, of the guards that protected Ruler and the Seat. Jabuticabron, Sass's big brother, wouldn't be out of place at this table. Aside from the red skin, amber eyes and black horns, that was.

"What I'm about to say," she told me with great intensity, "is treason simply by act of speaking."

I was listening.

"Not everyone," she hesitated before forging on, words rushed, "believes in the course our Master has placed us on." Again the quick glance upward. No response from DB. Coolio.

I waited for her to go on anyway. Didn't get anything further for a long moment. While it didn't surprise me Dark Brother discouraged original thought, knowing even speaking against him was a traitorous act made me sit up and take further notice.

"I'm in the presence of some of those, I take it?"

Hope, once a lie I told myself to feel better about a terrible situation, woke and waved her happy hands.

The commander nodded. "Nor do we believe the prophecy he has shared with us about you, Doombringer."

Wait a second. They kept calling me that. But I was the doom of my Universe. And yet, it was Belaisle who used that term, a tool of Dark Brother. Now I was confused.

"Prophecy?" First I'd heard of that. The one I knew was done, finished off when we defeated Belaisle and woke the Stronghold plane. They had a different one, it seemed.

Shonya didn't answer that query, at least not right away. "Our Master wishes to reclaim the other Universe," she said, "and right the wrong that split it from ours in the beginning of days."

Um, hang on. "You do know your Universe came second, right?"

She flinched, gritted her teeth, green sparks lighting in her gray eyes. "His desire," she went on as if I'd never spoken such sacrilege, "is to eliminate the foul magicks that came from the split and ruined your Universe, combining all into the one true power."

Sorcery.

"What about the *lóng*?" They had used those horrible powers at their disposal and Dark Brother didn't seem all that upset about using them. Blank looks met my question. "And the maji?" I hadn't seen them here then flinched as I realized what I'd said. Idiot. The maji weren't here, were they?

Nothing that was created after Max split sorcery into the different powers would exist here. Except the *lóng*, which convinced me further they didn't belong here. But this way of thinking would take some getting used to.

The Commander just glared at me. I guess she was having trouble with her own participation in this conversation. It had to be hard to face the truth despite wanting it in the first place. While choosing to doubt and question might seem reasonable in the face of supposition, it was an entirely different experience when the reality slapped you in the face.

"The second race," I murmured in way of explanation.

She just shrugged. "Then it's true?"

Oliver shifted beside me and I turned to find him watching her without humor at last. It was the first time I'd seen him without a grin on his face. He seemed even more familiar than ever. The shape of his jaw, the way his eyes crinkled at the corners when he spoke. But I didn't know him, I was sure of that.

"We've known," he said, quiet and calm. "The drach have never lied to us."

It was Mabel's turn to nod and sigh. "Though our vindication is far from our final desire," she said.

Oliver addressed me directly, gray eyes open and unguarded. "A small faction of the Order is tied to the few remaining drach and have been since the beginning." He gestured at Mabel. "Our bloodlines are woven together. It was they who first guided and trained us."

"Until the drachmor evolution and takeover." Who? Had to be their term for the *lóng*. Mabel said it like it was no big deal but Oliver's anger was apparent. Looked like I wasn't the only one who wore their emotions on their face.

"The clean terms the Master and the drachmor use to excuse the near genocide of your race." He addressed Mabel directly.

She shrugged again, sadness in her diamond eyes. "Something we could do nothing about," she said before turning her gaze to me. "Until now."

Was this about revenge? "I can't help you fight your own people," I said, hating to admit my weakness.

But the commander grunted, cutting me off. "Our rebellion is risky, to say the least," she said. "However, it is our task to undertake. No, you're here for another reason, Doombringer." She paused, fingers tapping a rhythm on the table before fisting in front of her, settling like a rock of flesh on the polished top. "Are you here to destroy our Universe at last?"

Loaded question. One I should have lied about because as I stared into the commander's eyes I saw my own end there in her fear and worry. If I was smart, I would have made up a story, found the means to make them trust me, help me win my freedom.

Instead, tired of the game and ready to face my fate, I exhaled.

"Yes," I said. "And."

THIRTY-ONE

I found myself explaining everything that was happening on the other side of the barrier between Universes. Despite the commander's frequent grimaces and occasional grunts of disbelief, I managed to wind my way through it all, from Gabriel's first opening of the Gateway here—they were shocked to discover Ameline was the baddie in my Universe—to rebuilding Creator's statue and all the trouble I'd been having doing so.

When I brought up Max, Mabel shifted her position, perking.

"I thought I knew him," she said, wonder in her voice even as the ribbon around my wrist tightened and something sparked in me, a terrible feeling much like grief. "He led us once, millennia ago. But he gave his life when Dark Brother allowed us to evolve into the drachmor."

"Not evolve," I corrected her as gently as I could while the other two stared at me. "Stole. From my Universe." I had to find out how Dark Brother brought them here. I was beginning to wonder if he had, or if they'd made their own way. Surely if they'd crossed under his power he could use that way against us. So, had this been Fate? My head hurt, as usual, when I thought of stupid ass destiny. "They control more than just sorcery. Don't they?"

The commander looked uncomfortable but Oliver nodded. "It's part of the reason they have dominated so long," he said, gesturing to Mabel. "There was a time the drach were our partners, our friends. But the creation," he corrected himself instantly, "arrival of the drachmor signaled the end of that. We never understood why, or could fathom their power. Now I see why that is." He shook his head, longish hair swaying around his ears, his high cheekbones. "And yet our own Master speaks against the abomination that is other magicks."

"Do as I say," I murmured, "not as I do." Oliver grunted in answer.

"Our people were enslaved, killed off by the drachmor," Mabel said, without a trace of anger or blame. Just stating drach fact, thank you, ma'am. "Our ability to fly and to transform into our natural shape is also gone." That left a flicker of regret behind and I felt my own heart clench for her. I remembered flying, taking drach form. Still missed it. Would have it again someday. Unlike poor Dark Mabel and her people.

What kind of sick bastard does that to an entire race?

Shonya leaped to her feet suddenly, pacing past the end of the table, big hands clasped behind her back. Distress pulled her full mouth down, puckered a line between her eyes that made me think of Mom and how terrified she'd be for me.

Damn it, I'd been out of my prison's shielding for ages and hadn't even tried to reach Gabriel. What was I thinking?

"Take her back to her cell." The commander wasn't going to give me a chance to correct my mistake. From the tight, frightened look on her face she'd decided it was better to follow orders after all. But Oliver stood up next to me, face grim, hands clenched at his sides, belying the calm of his voice when he answered her.

"No," he said, soft, gentle. "We will listen."

She was his commander. He was pushing his luck, right? But no, not so it seemed. She faltered, stood still, stared into his eyes with distress clear on her face. Then nodded, suddenly tired appearing, shoulders slumping, head down.

"The Universe forgive us," she said.

"I'm sure it will when this is over," Oliver said. "More than that, if Sydlynn is right, if Doombringer is telling the truth, which I believe she is," thanks for the vote of confidence, pretty boy, "it sounds as if it's our own Master who is driving the Universe to its destruction."

I hadn't thought of it that way. But no, I had to correct him. Didn't I?

Way to keep your damned fool mouth shut, Syd.

"I'm Doombringer, it's true." I wasn't about to try to get around that one. "But from what I know, I'm meant to bring the doom of my own Universe. And, I guess, drag you along with me."

"That's not how we've been taught," Oliver said, face suddenly unreadable. "Your very name is used as a curse, your face known to every single Order man, woman and child down through the generations. The destroyer of our Universe for your own perverse pleasures."

"Sounds like me," I said at my most sarcastic.

He grinned suddenly, going from serious soldier to happy-go-lucky kid in a flicker of an eye. Damn him, he really was delicious.

Syd, my vampire sighed. *Focus.*

Doesn't mean we can't enjoy the view, my demon sent.

Agreed, Shaylee breathed.

Seriously.

"As much as I wish I could comfort you in your time of worry," I said, "I'm afraid with every piece of Creator we return, the Universe fails further. Both of them, from what I've been told."

Shonya nodded brusquely as if to shake off her fears, something clearly uncharacteristic for her. "Our people have been disappearing," she said, "our Order's numbers dwindling as planes vanish. Into the void." She seemed stunned by the facts.

"And what about Fate?" I'd already been told whoever took over existed in this Universe, too.

They all looked uncomfortable a moment, though Mabel recovered first. "She's told us you must return to your own Universe, that you've received what you came for."

I did indeed. The glare the commander fixed on me made me a little nervous, but she didn't ask further questions despite the fact she had to be dying to interrogate me. Strength of will I could respect.

"Fate struggles to gain the attention of anyone," Oliver said, sounding faintly guilty. Did that include him? "We have orders to kill her if she's discovered."

Oops. "I take it that's one of your little rebellions then?"

The commander sighed. Question answered.

"I need to see her." Well, I didn't, not really. I needed to go home. But curiosity was killing me. Was it Zoe here, too?

I hadn't noticed the door behind the commander's chair, not until it eased open and a face I knew far too well appeared. But it wasn't the Helios Oracle, nor was it

Bellanca or Thanos. No, this person floored me so badly I bit my lower lip to keep from weeping at the sight.

I knew her, knew her well. Had known her, many years ago. Still missed her. I wished I could have saved her from the stake and the fire. Saved her estranged brother the agony of her loss just after they discovered each other again.

Instead, I stood and shook. Mia Dumont closed the door behind her and fixed me with her icy blue eyes.

"Hello, Doombringer," she said.

THIRTY-TWO

Mia. Alive. After all this time. But not my Mia, was she? Not the girl I first knew as Pain, the Goth friend I'd adored despite her penchant for crazy, to discover she was the long lost daughter of the Dumont family, her power locked away for so long it shattered her mind in the end.

Why did that make me think of Liam? Why did seeing her suddenly force to the surface a terrible hope that shouldn't be anywhere near the front of my mind right now?

I couldn't help myself as she strode into the room and came to my side to stare into my eyes like she knew me.

If Mia was alive in this Universe, if she had her own version of herself here, did that mean Liam was here, too? And, if so, could I find him? Bring him home with me?

Looking into her eyes, peering into the depths of the

soul of the woman that looked like my Mia, I felt my hope shrink and shrivel. This body might appear like my old friend. Might have her eyes and her high cheekbones and even the same voice, but it wasn't her. The woman who looked back at me out of that gaze was totally in control of herself and had been, I'd guess, her entire life.

Liam might be here. But he wouldn't know me. And he'd be a different person than the man I loved.

I blinked several times, forcing down tears as she observed me, head cocking to one side, shining black hair bobbed off at her chin so well known to me I wanted to stroke it back from her cheek.

"You look the same as her," she said, as if mirroring my thoughts. "And you sound the same. But you're nothing like Sydlynn Hayle of our Universe."

At least I'd still been a Hayle here and not a Dumont. I don't think I could have handled it knowing the me of this Universe had been raised by Odette and her ilk.

Just shudder.

"You've been listening." Not sure why that statement was all I could muster, but I was proud of myself for managing to sound at least partially in control.

She nodded, smiled, rueful and playful. "I have," she said. "I find it's safer to observe first and poke my nose in later." Trouble lived in that icy gaze, worry she hid well. "Let me ask you if your Fate is the same person as you see before you?"

I shook my head. "She's not," I said. Almost blurted the truth but kept my tongue. From the tightening of her smile, her faint nod, she understood my silence for what it was.

"I see," she said.

"Did you depose anyone to take your place?" She'd asked, so I wanted answers of my own. It made no sense Bellanca and Thanos would be here, too, as Fates, if only because there were no maji. But she nodded.

"A pair of twins," she said, flicking her fingers as if they didn't matter. "It was time. They were *his* tools and it seems our Universe needed someone a bit more… outspoken."

"She means honest," Oliver said with a grin.

Mia shrugged her thin shoulders, teeth flashing white against her red lips. "How about *practical?*"

"And this happened when? About six months ago?"

She nodded, eyes tightening a bit, lower lip sucking in as she watched me carefully.

The timing was exactly the same as Zoe's. Okay then. Not sure why that reassured me, but I was happy to know the Universes were in sync.

"Your Fate too, I imagine?" She turned away from me, arms crossing over her chest, meeting Shonya's gaze. "And still you doubt me, Commander?"

The tall redhead shrugged. "I've come this far with you, Fate," she said.

Mia tossed her head, flashing me her blue eyed gaze like we were coconspirators in some fashion. Her demeanor said, "As if." I almost smiled even as sadness washed over me. This is who Mia Dumont was supposed to be. Had never had the chance to grow into. How tragic, her loss, when such potential lived in her heart.

If Mia had lived, would she have taken Zoe's place? No way of knowing. And it didn't matter, did it? She was dead and I wasn't exactly in a position to figure out what ifs at the moment. Though it was exactly the kind of pondering Max would love to contemplate and talk out over a long evening at the Stronghold.

Max. I had to find him. How had I forgotten he was in as much danger—maybe more—than I was? My gaze flickered over Mabel and my stomach clenched. Sudden urgency hit me in hard and made me focus.

"I have to go home." Blurty pants much? They all looked at me like I was supposed to say more. "The fate of everything depends on it." Okay, I was reaching. But the heart in my pocket told me otherwise. I needed to return it.

Mia nodded in answer. "Agreed," she said, though she addressed that word to the commander who flinched and looked away. "No arguments, Shonya. What has been begun must be completed or we all pay the price."

Now she sounded like Fate. "Do you know where this is going?"

Mia's face flattened, stilled. "You know I can't tell you anything, so don't ask."

Sigh. "At least tell me if you know what's happening on my side."

She grinned suddenly. "I bet your Fate just loves you."

I laughed this time, unable to stop myself. "We have our moments," I said.

"All I know," Mia said, arms dropping to her sides, voice deepening—was that the Universe talking through her as she went on?—"is that the fate of everything can't be decided here. There is much more to come and if the Doombringer isn't allowed to leave with what she came for, we're all done." She fixed the commander with a hard glare. "All of us, both Universes. And there will be no coming back from it."

"What did you come for?" Shonya turned her attention to me, surprise in her voice before it steadied, as if shocked she'd not thought to ask. I wondered how much Fate had to do with her lack of interest in my quest. Surely a woman like her, one who'd made it so far in the Order, was accustomed to finding out truths from those who didn't want to share it.

Tell them, Mia's voice echoed in my head. *One way or another, you're getting out of here. I have the power to see to it.* She didn't sound completely confident, but it was enough I drew the small, plastic toy from my pocket and held out my hand, palm up. The red heart quivered in my grasp, rocking slightly before settling. It looked like nothing, and yet, it was everything.

Everything.

"This," I said. "The pieces of Creator I mentioned? This is one of them."

Shonya looked suspicious, even scornful. "That's nothing."

"Look closer." I let her see what I saw, the shimmering outline of Creator's true heart around it. She peered at it before falling back with a cry, turning away.

"Please," the commander gasped. "Don't do that."

I glanced at Mia who shrugged, noticing then Oliver seemed uncomfortable, though Mabel stared with an intensity that worried me. Covetous need flashed over her face even as I closed my hand and put the heart away.

"Why didn't Dark Brother detect it?" Leave it to Oliver to ask the question I didn't have a real answer to. I shrugged and pointed at the ribbon on my wrist.

"Whether it was Creator Herself or this drach soul, he didn't seem to know or maybe to care I carried it." Still weird.

Mabel frowned, came forward, hand outstretched and I allowed her to touch the ribbon. It flexed at her attention while she stared down at it, intensity almost as powerful as when she observed the heart. For a moment I worried she might try to take it from me, but when she finally backed away, she sighed in sadness, diamond eyes meeting mine.

"I know that soul," she said. "He is faithful. You can trust him with your life."

Considering he'd proven himself over and over, I was happy enough for the confirmation even if it was unnecessary at this point. "Who is he?"

She didn't say, gaze sharp and sad. And when she turned away, I let her go.

Whoever it was, I was grateful to have him.

"So why is the heart here?" Oliver and his to the point questions. I'd underestimated him from the moment I'd met him, distracted by his handsome face, by the smirk that irritated me and reminded me of Quaid, for some reason. Maybe that's why he pissed me off. My ex had when we'd first met, too. "If it's from your Universe, how did it end up in our back yard?"

I didn't bother telling them about Trill, not when Mia spoke up.

"Does it matter?" She didn't seem worried by the fact. "For whatever reason, Syd had to come here. And now she's here, she has what she needs and has to go home again."

I was puzzled too. This seemed like a fool's errand, a journey across the Universes for what? I hated unanswered questions.

"There is an order to everything," she said, giving me

chills, "and to everything an order." Channeling Zoe now, was she? Mia tipped her head to me. "You've done what you need to do, Doombringer. Time to go."

Wait, hang on a second. "Awesome," I said, "thanks for the hospitality, happy to get out of Dodge, but there's one small thing first. Just a trifle, really." They watched me in confused silence as my anger flashed back through my sarcasm and came out in a snarl. "I'm not sure about loyalty and faithfulness in this Universe, but there's no way in hell I'm leaving without my friends." Well, friend. Hadn't Jiao betrayed me? Or had she? More questions, no answers.

Even Oliver lost his cockiness. "The drach," he said, cheeks paling, eyes wide as he swallowed past something that didn't agree with him.

Not a good sign. And even more reason to go into rescue mode. "Hell, yeah," I snapped. "Where is Max?"

THIRTY-THREE

"I'm sorry," the commander said, exactly the wrong words to come out of her mouth. "It's impossible. You have to go without him."

She clearly had a different definition of impossible than I did. "I'm not leaving," I said in no uncertain terms, "without Max."

So there, Order lady. Take that.

Before the big, burly woman could express her unhappiness with my statement, Oliver leaned closer to me and addressed her over my shoulder.

"I'll take her," he said.

Shonya's face crumpled, terror in her eyes. "Absolutely not. If they catch you, they'll kill you."

He nodded, shrugged. "We're in this completely or not at all."

"I can get them close." Mabel shivered faintly but

seemed determined. At what cost to her? Did I dare ask or would it make me hesitate when I couldn't afford to? Way to put other people in harm's way for the sake of your friends, Hayle. And yet, that was the story of my life. Besides, I was doing the same to me, wasn't I? Weird to suddenly think of Shenka and her accusation I only had tools in place of people I cared about. But, did I ever ask others to do what I myself wasn't willing to?

That was a big noperino. Made me feel better. And stand a little taller.

Mia's face had darkened, but she nodded her agreement. "The drach must return with you," she said, cutting off any further protest from the commander of the Order. The big woman finally sagged and gave up the fight.

"Be careful," she said. Another ping in my soul, this time unexpected. As I turned to Oliver to ask him his plan, I had an acute about face when it came to my thoughts about the Order. I'd been so afraid of them, of the marching terror they'd become in my head since the day my son opened a Gateway and almost let them through. But here they were, proving to me they were as real, had deep emotional lives and an existence just as I did. As those I loved did. Made hating them harder.

Okay then. Dark Brother I could hate. We'd leave it at that then, right? Everything I did from here was for the good of all of us in both Universes.

Well, with a couple of exceptions. Belaisle and Eva Southway could kiss my ass.

I didn't get to ask the Order soldier what he had in mind. Seconds later, after saluting his commander, Oliver spun and headed for the exit, forcing me to follow. I turned at the door, Shonya with her back to me, Mia smiling and waving as if I were headed out on a field trip. I waved back, wished I'd taken a moment to hug her. Sure, she wasn't the same woman, but it would have been nice to do so, just one more time.

Instead, with Oliver leading and Mabel at my back, I stepped out into the hallway and uncertain fate.

No, not uncertain. I would find Max, I would reach Gabriel and we would make it home to return Creator's heart. I would. There were no options otherwise. I hadn't come this far, endured what I'd endured, just to fail.

Keep telling yourself that, Syd.

My demon snorted a laugh at my internal dialogue, but kept her thoughts to herself. Smart of her.

"She's worried about you." It felt weird to march down the stone hallway in total silence. Still, even as I opened my mouth I wondered if talking was allowed between guards and prisoners. Sure, we were alone, as far as I knew. But my usual running commentary might blow our cover.

Oliver hadn't replaced his helmet, carrying it under his right arm. He glanced back at me with a grin and some sadness in his eyes.

"I know," he said. "Doesn't matter how old I get. Don't think it ever will." His cheeks pinked faintly and he turned away again. "My own fault, I guess. I've always been the rebellious child."

Wait, what?

"Oliver is the commander's youngest son," Mabel whispered over my shoulder.

And now it all made total sense.

My guide/guard paused a moment, slipping his helmet into place at last. When he was done, I shivered at the shining hulk of metal he'd transformed into once again, the cold and lifeless faceplate covering his handsome features. But the jaunty way he gestured for me to follow him through the door at the end of the hall reassured me. I did as I was told without a word.

Nice to have Mabel at my back, even if she wasn't really my Mabel and had been parted from her wings in a most violent and unforgivable act. Something I'd never, ever share with my drach ancestress. I had no doubt, if she knew what happened, it would break her giant heart.

I wasn't prepared for the wide space we entered and gaped in shock as we crossed the far corner of an enormous room—that term being the only one I had to describe the giant cafeteria style and bench and table filled square far outstripping the massive one I knew at the Stronghold. And yet, as we quickly crossed without challenge toward another set of doors, I took tally of the bodies in the room, the echoing empty feeling of it, and wondered if maybe we were here at an off time.

Or, more hopefully, that the ranks of the Order had been reduced to the small number of armor clad folk who rattled around inside the massive space.

I missed completely the fact we were being approached due to my instinctual head counting, only noticing the three *lóng* who stopped us when I jerked to a halt thanks to Mabel's hand on the back of my shirt. I gaped at the trio, realizing they were the same ones who we'd passed in the hallway on our way to see Shonya.

The lead female with her heavy blonde braid eyed me with suspicion. "Where are you taking the prisoner?"

Mabel hurried forward before Oliver could speak and to my utter horror prostrated herself before the *lóng* with her face pressed to the woman's legs.

"I beg you, mistress," Mabel said in a quavering voice. "My daughter. Have you chosen her sentence?"

Oliver moved on as if the three hadn't stopped us at all and I marched beside him, his gauntleted hand grasping my arm and pulling me roughly along. We left Mabel behind, my heart aching for her as she sobbed and the three *lóng* —distracted so easily by their new toy— laughed at her suffering.

We exited the big room without anyone else saying a thing and I exhaled in relief when the door closed behind us. Another black stone hallway, much like the first, empty and extending out into the distance.

"We should be all right for a few minutes," Oliver said, voice hollow behind his helmet. "But it will get hairy when we enter the drachmor cavern."

"Drachmor?" That wasn't the first time I'd heard that term, but was the first chance I had to ask.

He nodded. "You call them *lóng*," he said, confirming the connection I'd already made. "But we know them as drachmor."

I had to think about it for a second before rolling my eyes at the arrogance of it. Drach *more*. More than drach. Classy.

I had a huge question though, as we continued along the hallway. One that bothered me immensely. "This is too easy," I said. "Why isn't anyone else bothered by the fact Doombringer is out and about with a single Order soldier as a guard?"

Now who was arrogant? Still, it seemed a logical question.

Oliver didn't laugh or, at least, I didn't hear it. But there was definite humor in his voice when he answered.

"You might be Doombringer," he said, "but no one challenges the Order. And no Order soldier goes against our Master."

Except him and his mom. How precious.

Sydlynn. Mabel's mind reached mine, distant and sad.

Trust the drach soul you carry. And save your friend. I wish I could have done so for the same one here.

Something in the way she said it made cogs turn. *Are you saying what I think you're saying?* Impossible. And yet, all along I'd wondered why the drach soul in my possession—okay, who'd taken ownership of me—I so readily accepted.

Be safe, she sent. *And save us all.*

No pressure or anything. Her mind left mine before I could prod her further and I sent her silent farewell. Maybe when this was done she could get her wings back.

Fairy tales came true sometimes.

Speaking of the ribbon, it flexed and spun as we approached the far door and I realized why when Oliver paused with his hand flat, pressed to the wood. "Their territory isn't the same as ours," he said. "We'll have to move fast."

Or stealthy. I could feel the press of power beyond the portal, knew we were walking into a situation far less relaxed—if I could call it that—than the one the Order allowed. They might be full of themselves in believing I wasn't a threat. But the *lóng*—the drachmor, I corrected myself—weren't so foolish.

The black ribbon shifted again, triggering my white sorcery. And, instantly, I had an idea. And kicked myself silently for not thinking of it before.

"Rather than just waltzing into danger," I said, "how

about a disguise?" I reached into my memory for the image of the *lóng* bodyguards that used to stand beside Moa, the vampire Empress. Their faces were familiar enough and their Chinese dragon forms just as much thanks to my repeated exposure to Jiao. Maybe we wouldn't pass careful scrutiny, but I'd figured out enough playing with Sass's physical form I could at least create an illusion that would hold up.

Or so I told myself. Oliver's tall, shining form shifted in my view from hulking Order soldier to slim, almond eyed dangerousness. Those eyes widened, flickering with panic as his new form settled around him.

"What power is that?" He shivered, as if trying to shake off the lean shape, the *lóng* he appeared rippling in my second sight. It would do.

Ah, right. "Something you don't have to worry about," I said. "Unless this goes badly. Then, well. I'll tell you about it if they let us live long enough."

"Looking forward to it," he said, even as he flinched and glanced back the way we'd come.

"What?" I felt a mustache move on my upper lip, twitched it in irritation. I had to pick the one with the facial hair.

He shrugged, dark eyes narrowing. "They know you're missing," he said. "We'd better hurry." And, instead of trying to lead me away or argue with me how dangerous this was, he opened the door and went in search of my friend.

No matter what happened from here on in, Oliver had my respect. And my thanks.

Into the dragon's lair, quite literally. I practiced my "don't mess with me" Jiao/Charlotte/crankass face, ignoring the two drachmor we passed the instant we entered their domain. This part of the mountain was rougher hewn but bubbled with magic, as if the very rock housed the power of the drach evolution. Without time to even hope we might fool them, I exhaled a moment later, Oliver striding confidently at my side with a sultry swing to his now narrow hips.

"I could use a trick like this," he said, odd hearing his voice emerging from the *lóng*'s mouth.

The corridor wasn't deep, ending quickly in a vast cavern I recognized. This was where they'd taken us when we'd first been captured. The stalagmites and stalactites perches of a few drachmor were, I could only guess, the real homes of the species. So weird to see all the different kinds of them wheeling above, going about their business. Hard not to stare. I had to remind myself I was under cover a few times and jerk my gaze forward.

If this wasn't so scary and stupid and risky, I'd be really enjoying the view.

Why aren't they reacting to my escape? I aimed that question as tightly as I could.

Oliver's dark head tipped slightly in my direction. *My*

mother is doing her best to keep our "disgrace" to the Order for now, he sent. *She's browbeating our people into finding you. But the drachmor will be alerted shortly, I assure you. We have to hurry.*

He didn't have to encourage me or anything. With sure strides and a deadly manner I coveted, Oliver crossed the large cavern and led me to a set of stairs. Down we descended deeper underground. It reminded me too much of the staircase to my own prison and I had to wipe at beads of sweat on my upper lip, wetting my mustache. Ew. How did guys handle facial hair? Great thing to be thinking about when visions of my guide betraying me made my heart pound. I was in a frazzled lather when he stopped at last at the far end of the rough-hewn tunnel and spun open the heavy, metal door.

Oliver didn't speak, unsealing the portal with a whisper of power and stepping through to the other side, leaving me to follow. Heart clenched against what might wait for me, I joined him, pulling the door shut behind me.

No Max, just a pit leading down into darkness. I peered over the edge, my vertigo kicking in. But I caught sight of a gray tail, a claw and forgot in that instant I was afraid of heights. Sorcery lowered me into the hole, my mind at least collected enough I remembered to use the power of this Universe. I had no idea if the elemental magicks inside me would trigger some kind of response so I couldn't risk it.

My knees hit the hard rock when I collapsed onto them next to the lump of what had been my friend, a sob escaping me as I took in what they had done to him. Giant head bleeding from several places, a long, narrow bank of claw marks across his wide ribs. A deep slice into his tail, multiple wounds weeping blood. But none of that was the worst of his injuries, all of it I knew he could heal with time and help.

Alive, he was alive. But maybe he didn't want to be anymore. I leaned in and touched his drach face with my shaking hands, letting my old appearance emerge as I whispered his name and did my best not to stare at the two charred, empty lumps over his shoulders.

Max's wings were gone.

THIRTY-FOUR

The black ribbon on my wrist flexed in sympathy as I pressed my forehead against Max's muzzle, tears streaming down my face. He was warm at least, not the icy cold of death, though I feared he was close to it after all. When I finally lifted my head, his diamond eye opened and fixed on me.

"Syd," he whispered, musical voice harsh and heavy, his normally fresh, spring like breath full of decay.

"I'll kill them for this." My rage rose in a fiery wave, my demon howling inside me, Shaylee shaking the ground beneath us. But it was the black ribbon on my wrist that pulled me out of my anger. It slipped from my skin and wound itself around Max's brow ridge, humming softly to him while his big eye closed again.

Syd, my vampire sent, her grief as heavy as mine. *We*

have to get out of here. Or we'll lose him.

Agreed. And here I was wasting my energy on anger. I surged to my feet, turned to find my magical transformation of Oliver had ended when my own fell away. He stood staring at Max with regret, though his fear was palpable at last.

"If you're going to escape," he said, voice tight, gaze turning upward to the cell above, "I suggest you get at it."

I heard them then, the shrieking of the drachmor. They knew. They were coming.

Let them come. We'd be long gone before they came near. And I'd not be saving their asses when the time came, you'd better believe it. The bloody drachmor could burn in hell for what they'd done right along with their damned Dark Brother master.

I reached for Gabriel, for the veil, diving into it even as power hit the door upstairs. It was only then I realized Oliver had barred the way, made time for me to escape. I stared at him while my mind cried out for my son with all the magic I had.

Oliver's mother was right. I was going to get him killed.

"Syd," Max's voice reached me as I screamed again for Gabriel, fought the veil for any sign my son heard me. Nothing, just emptiness. This veil didn't know me, didn't want me here. It fought me, struggling against me and, as it did, I felt him coming. Felt his awareness roused by my cries, his attention drawn. And panic kicked me hard in the heart.

Dark Brother. He was coming. I had to reach Gabriel. Now.

"Syd." Again Max called to me. I turned, desperate and terrified. "Leave me."

Oh, *hell* no. "If I could find a way out," I snapped at him, "I'd consider it. Now shut up and let me work here." I drew on my white sorcery, threw it at the veil. Again I was repelled, the rubbery membrane of this Universe absorbing my magic for its own.

Damn it, I thought I was supposed to go home. I spun toward Oliver, saw his grim determination past his fear, watched a flaming sword appear in his hands, almost as tall as he was. The dark orange glow pulsed with the icy blue of the hottest fire as he took a step toward me before turning, creating a barrier between me and Max and what was coming for us above.

"It's been a pleasure," he said. "Now get the hell out of here and let me die for you already."

"You have a death wish?" I cast about me in need, in growing despair, knowing we were all lost after all, that Fate was wrong and Trill betrayed me to die here, torn apart by Dark Brother and the drachmor.

Oliver shrugged, armor catching fire as the door above burst inward, showering us with fragments and the sound of wings deafened me. *At least I finally did something,* he sent.

No way could I let such strength of will go to waste.

Turned out, it wasn't my job in the end. Something clamped around my wrist and, tying itself firmly to my magic, pushed me headlong into the darkness of the veil.

The black ribbon, the soul of the drach, flew beside me, vague form taking shape next to me as it did. That spirit and its power the veil recognized, withdrawing reluctantly, giving me the gap I needed to call out to my son at last.

To find the doorway Trill had left behind. Even as a beloved face smiled at me just as the black ribbon's mortal form vanished into the twitching thing around my wrist. Fresh tears trickled as I realized the truth while a mind I loved more than life itself grasped onto mine and screamed.

MOM!

I fell back into myself, having never really been in the veil, only my conscious mind gone to that place. Pressure compressed the world around me, pushing me down toward the rock, toward Max's prone form while the blazing armor of the Order soldier before me held the darkness at bay long enough for my son to get through. For a Gateway to form.

I shoved Max into it with all my strength, my magic hurtling him past the entry and across the Universe. He, at least, would survive. Something slammed into my back, driving me to my knees, and I turned in time to find the blonde drachmor woman standing over me while Oliver was swarmed with power.

Jiao appeared at her side, smiling at me. "Mistress," my former friend said to the blonde before turning her with an efficient grasp and punching the woman full in the face.

Now. Jiao grasped me by one arm and threw me at the Gateway, her own slim body pursing mine. But as I fell through, my shoulders hitting the edge, I saw Oliver go down and knew I couldn't just let him die. He'd saved my life, risked everything for a Fate he trusted. And his mother's fear... I knew a mother's fear.

Zoe's voice sounded loud in my head, though it was only a memory. *When you meet him, you will know him.*

White sorcery lashed out in a flash of instinct, enough to part the drachmor from him, enough to latch onto his flaming armor and pull.

And then we were falling and the way was darkness, spinning madness, the veil a spitting, snarling creature until I felt myself split and pivot, embraced by a love I knew well, the welcoming warmth of the veil on my side. An instant later I was out, crashing to the ground in the grass of my backyard in Wilding Springs.

Oliver hit me with his full weight, falling on top of me, armor still hot from the fire. He rolled over instantly, the metal encasing his body ringing with the impact. I gasped in a breath to lungs knocked empty by the landing, choking on the fresh air a moment.

Home.

Dear elements, were we really home?

A small, vibrating bundle slammed into me and hugged me around my neck, squeezing so hard I lost my breath a second time. "Mom," he whispered over and over again. "Mom!"

I hated to push him free, but fear won the war for my attention and I found myself screaming in my head for the one person I knew could help. *MABEL!*

She came, she and a handful of drach, appearing instantly in the yard, hovering around Max. He'd managed to half change himself into partial drach/human form, though his missing wings were obvious, the spaces behind his shoulders blackened and weeping cloudy ichor. Mabel didn't say anything, though her sadness at his condition told me what I needed to know.

"Will he be okay?" I choked on the fear I'd gotten my friend killed when the other drach took Max away, leaving the tall, beautiful woman whose bloodline I carried behind.

"He will live," she said, voice shaking with emotion. "Because you brought him home to us."

"His wings." I sobbed the words. "Mabel."

She nodded, suddenly firm and in control. "Can be regrown," she said. "Leave his care to us. For now, you have what you went for?"

My hand went protectively to my right pocket, the lump of plastic. "I do," I said, unable to muster enthusiasm into my dull voice.

"All is well then," she said, though her eyes widened as she stared over my shoulder and I knew what she looked at before I even turned with a sigh to examine the tall, shining man in full armor in my backyard. The least he could do was stop smoking, puffs of the now silent fire he'd called escaping in little bouts from the creases of his metal plating as he planted himself at attention.

Showoff.

But I didn't address Oliver yet, not when Jiao came to me, embraced me. I hugged her back, not knowing what to do or say.

I would never betray you, she sent. *Never.* Such fierceness in her. She leaned away, stared into my eyes. *We have much to discuss, a great deal of intel to share. They are evil, Syd. And must be stopped at all costs.*

She left me alone then, turning to slip into the arms of the young man who watched me with fearful eyes. Sassafras embraced her without shame or hesitation and confirmed what I already knew. A couple then. Good for them.

My fingers stroked over the black ribbon around my wrist, the epiphany I'd had about it—about him—returning while the air in my yard burst and erupted with tunnels, with blue fire, people arriving to stop and stare at me in mute silence as they landed in a rush. Stunned and shell shocked by my appearance. No, not at mine.

At the Order soldier in his full armor who waited for me to notice him.

"You shouldn't have brought me here," he said, pulling his helmet free as if we were alone. So much guilt on his face smudged with ash, so much regret.

"I couldn't leave you to die." Zoe's voice again, the memory of her prophecy. Was he part of the reason I had to go to the other Universe? But why? Maybe a chance to study the Order would give us an advantage. But even my cynical mind wasn't convinced. There was more to this—to him—than I'd allowed myself to believe just yet.

We'd see.

"You realize you've made a terrible mistake." Oliver sighed, shrugged.

"You're welcome." And the snarky smartass returned. Awesome. Nice to be her again.

He shook his head. "You don't understand," he said. "Now that I'm here..." he looked around as if wondering despite himself where "here" was exactly. "They've been looking for a way to cross for a long time. Wanted to know how you managed it."

"Good luck finding a way without my son." I pulled Gabriel toward me, against me. "He's the Gateway."

Oliver didn't seem impressed by what I'd just said.

"Syd," he said. "You have to send me back. Right now."

"They'll kill you." Why did that matter to me? Because he'd risked everything to save me. I wasn't about to put him back into the line of fire. "I'm sorry, but you're stuck with us until this is over." I guess I'd be kind of pissed to have to sit things out too if I was suddenly in the other Universe with no way home.

Oliver's gray eyes glinted with hints of green as he spoke. "Syd," he said. "I wish it was that easy. But you've just given them the path they needed." I froze, finally understanding what he was so afraid of. "I won't have to go home for them to find me and kill me." He looked up at the sky, inhaled heavily, exhaled. "In fact, unless something drastic stopped them," he sounded like that was impossible, "they're already here."

I gaped at him.

"They just needed someone to follow," Oliver said with gentleness I clearly didn't deserve. "And you gave that to them."

THIRTY-FIVE

I would have given up there and then, tossed in the towel knowing what I'd done. All but for my son who smiled up at the grim and worried Order soldier and shook his blond head.

"No," he said with such surety I instantly believed him over Oliver's fear. "I am the Gateway and for as long as the veil holds and the Universe remains, I won't allow it."

And in that instant, holding my son against me like the boy I still thought of him, I understood at last just how gigantic my kid was. How huge and all encompassing, how Universal. That he could simply stop the Order from coming to our side of things with a simple decision to make it so.

Proud Mama right here. Terrified, shaken. But proud.

Oliver knelt before my son and smiled at him. "So you're the Gateway," he said before looking up at me and winking. "Stealth mode?"

I had to laugh. No other option seemed to fit. "I learned from the best."

And while I was sure Gabriel had no idea what we were talking about, he smiled too and my world was all right again.

It was only then I remembered the yard was full of people who hovered, anxious to see us, to find out what the hell happened. I smiled with a dazed feeling at my mother and Gram, next to whom stood a happy man with a cherub face and curling white hair.

"Demetrius!" I lunged for him, hugged him, seeing Piers then, the beaming smile on his face.

"You did it, Syd," he said, voice wavering, tears in his eyes. I released Demetrius, a small hand firmly holding mine when I stepped back. Piers grinned down at Gabriel, reached out as if to ruffle his hair and thought better of it. "You both did."

"I don't understand." Demetrius felt clean, not a trace of the Brotherhood in him. "What happened?"

"When we replaced the piece," my son said. "Everything started reverting, Mom. All sorcery finally reset back to the way it was supposed to be. No alliances, no camps. Just the power that was and the power that will be."

Control over sorcery. That was how Jean Marc was able to steal the Steam Union for his own, using the arm of Creator to do it. But if no one was affiliated with anyone anymore, that meant freedom for all sorcerers. "So putting the piece back removed their influence?"

Piers shrugged like he didn't understand it. I was beginning to, the edges of it. Each piece wasn't just in order, it had a connection, didn't it? To the different magicks of our Universe. Not only were they pulling the planes into the void, they were drawing the magic tied to them along for the ride. I was the only one, it seemed, who was able to maintain the powers that were vanishing into the void. Me and, from the magic pulsing inside him, my son.

You're learning, Gabriel sent, the veil in his eyes. *The order. It's important. More important than you know.*

I let it go in favor of happy hugs and welcome homes and the excitement of our success, despite knowing we had a long way to go. But having reassurance this was supposed to happen... well, I'd accept that as a win just to give me a bit of time to not feel like everything was falling apart and it was my fault. Peripheral me clung to two things I had to handle, though. One loomed in a corner of the yard in his shining armor, watching at a distance, looking out of place but willing to wait. And the other clung to my wrist in a band of black ribbon that was the soul of a drach I both didn't know at all and loved desperately.

"So no more Brotherhood." We'd finally migrated inside and I found myself sitting at the kitchen table with a coffee in my hand, munching cookies while the packed space spilled over with my family and friends.

Piers grimaced, though he looked the most relaxed I'd seen him in ages. "And no more Steam Union," he said, though he instantly waved off my shocked protest. "It's all good," he said. "We're figuring it out. And, to be honest, I'll take it."

Demetrius nodded with a happy smile. Okay then. Let them work things out.

"How long?" I had a vague inkling we'd been gone at least two days, but had no idea for sure.

"A week." Gabriel perched next to me, clinging to my hand. He hadn't let me go yet. The only real disappointment was my daughter's refusal to come out of her room, to hug me or talk to me or even acknowledge my presence. Fair enough. I'd left Ethie behind once too often, made her secondary to the things I needed to do. I could only imagine how hard that had to be for her. I'd find a time in the near future to be alone with her—just the two of us—and let her beat me up over it. For now, she could have her hissy fit.

Who was I to judge her?

It took me a second to process what Gabriel said. Wait a minute. I shook my head, sighed. A week. How long had I lost to Dark Brother's inquest? So much time. I did my best not to linger over the days gone and deliberately sipped my coffee.

"Are you going to tell us what happened?" Mom fidgeted in her chair, gaze drifting nervously to Oliver. At least she hadn't called him out as the enemy they had to all be thinking he was. Not yet, anyway. I was sure she was holding that in reserve for later. But it was Varity who grumped and sat back with her arms crossed over her chest.

"She'd rather keep us in the dark," the old Enforcer leader said with a wink.

She had no idea.

I took a moment to gather my thoughts, realizing as I did the room felt different, the people in it far more connected to me than ever before. And, with a quick check through as to why, gasped and looked up.

"You all have it now." They'd been sharing while I was away, clearly, the white sorcery their mutual connector.

"Thought it would come in handy if." Gram shrugged. No telling what "if" meant. Not when Gabriel's hand tightened on mine.

"Don't tell me you were going to come after me." Idiots.

They all grinned, murmured denials. Terrible liars, the lot of them.

When Oliver spoke up, I twitched. For a moment, I'd forgotten he was even there. But it was hard to miss him and his metal suit standing in the doorway to the kitchen, the way every pair of eyes locked on him after avoiding looking in his direction. Like they could pretend he wasn't the elephant in the room. I almost laughed at their nervousness, the way they perched so precariously on the edge of panic despite his quiet demeanor.

To be fair, they didn't know him like I did. Like I knew him at all. Except anyone who would willingly sacrifice themselves to save me had to have some good in them, right?

Right.

"You're talking about that power you used on me," Oliver said, wonder in his voice. "What is it?"

"Let me show you," Gabriel said. And before I could stop him, before Mom's gasp of fear or Piers's soft cry of denial could put an end to the idea, my son leaned over and touched Oliver's answering outstretched hand. A flare of white and the pale flames raced over him, diving down into the base of his feet. Oliver's armor shone like a star for an instant, so bright we all had to look away. When I finally turned back, it was to the most amazing smile on his face.

"That's…" he shook his head, smiling at me, his soul in his eyes. Clean, white, joyful.

"The true evolution of all power in the Universe,"

280

Gabriel said like it was no big deal as my family and friends stared in utter horror. "Cookie?"

They finally left me when I insisted, departing for their own continuing problems with hugs and love and relief at our return though I know a few would have liked to stay. To keep an eye on Oliver, no doubt, despite their fading fear of him.

Mom's was the most powerful embrace, her anxiety showing through as she let me go at last. *Syd*, she sent. *Are we safe having him here? Like this...?* She couldn't seem to go further, to grasp the words she needed beyond her deep and crushing concern for me. For all of us.

"We'll talk," I said. "I promise. I just need a shower and a change of clothes and I'm good to go."

She laughed, her fear fading as she touched my cheek with one shaking hand. "Syd," she said. "Can you trust him?"

No need asking who she was talking about. "We have to, Mom," I said even as I wondered then felt guilty for considering it. "Fate does."

She didn't say anything but I knew she'd do enough worrying for the both of us.

The fact my son had given an Order soldier the power he needed to defeat us if he ever managed to share it with his people didn't freak me out. Not at all.

Okay, a little bit. Yeah, a whole lot. Still.

Sigh.

I took my son's hand, unsurprised when Oliver joined us on our journey to the Stronghold. I let Sass glare at the still armored soldier as the cat in man form held his *lóng* girlfriend's hand all the way there. I'd done enough angsting in the last little while to last me.

Piers was right. It was all good.

Oliver stood silently beside me, an unreadable look on his face when Gabriel finally returned Creator's heart. He accepted the small, plastic toy into his hands, its transformation instant when it touched his skin. I felt it leave me, let it go when he crossed the stone floor and climbed into Creator's lap.

"This is what the Master is truly afraid of." Oliver's whisper might not have been meant for me, but I glanced at him where he stared down at his bare hands, his gauntlets tucked into his helmet at his feet. When he looked into my eyes, there was wonder there and I knew he didn't mean Gabriel's action. "This power, Syd. This is the truth." He let me feel him, did it on purpose, linking our magic together. I didn't stop him in time, felt the connection form between us, similar to that I'd always held for my loved ones. The connections I'd once severed and had rebonded on their own. I barely knew this man, and yet, in that moment, knew in my soul it was the right thing to do.

Yes, I could trust him. With anything.

I reached out on impulse and grasped his arm when the Stronghold shook at the placement of the heart. It was violent this time, much more so than ever and I did my best to ignore the collapse of the veil as it cried out in pain at its own dissolution. I couldn't help so I instead held rigid next to the man who should have been my mortal enemy and simply stood witness to the rapidly approaching end of everything, our magic supporting each other.

Two pieces left. The eyes and Creator's soul. It was only going to get worse. I couldn't even imagine.

Gabriel rejoined us, the Universe in his gaze. I hugged him, though he seemed at peace with what he was doing. Some comfort, at least.

We left the statue as a group when the shaking was done, when the veil finally settled into its new and reduced form. There was someone I needed to see, reminded keenly as the drach soul who guarded the heart rose behind me, whispering his joy at his freedom. Who was he? Didn't matter now. The one who needed to bear witness to his return had fallen. And right now I just wanted to see Max. To reassure myself I'd done the right thing letting him come with me.

Mabel showed us to the chamber where Max rested, a swarm of drach feeding him power as they sang to him the song of their people. I left Gabriel and Oliver, Sass and Jiao at the entry and strode inside, feeling as I did a presence stir and reach for me.

Light One. The Stronghold's voice was as slow and deep as ever, eternity in his tone. *I've been sleeping.* He sounded irritated at the fact.

You have. It was nice to know he was back, that he hadn't rebooted or anything. Or disappeared with the return of the heart. *How was it?*

Boring, he sent. *I've slept long enough. What has happened to the drach lord?*

I showed him what we'd done as best I could as the Stronghold's personality firmed up and woke the rest of the way.

I will assist, he sent with the firmness of stone. Power pulsed from the very structure and into Max in visible threads. The drach looked shocked by the help but their song never wavered. *He will live.* By sheer force of the Stronghold's will, apparently. Excellent.

Thank you. I wiped at fresh tears as the drach parted and let me through. Max was in full dragon form, his wings still gone, though the charred stumps were pink and pale grey. The ichor running was no longer yellowish and sickly but clear. Maybe there was hope for the other Mabel and her people. If things worked out.

They'd better damned well work out.

The ribbon on my wrist flexed as I bent over Max's big head and kissed his muzzle. "Scared me," I whispered over his scales.

"Thank you for not leaving me behind." His voice was soft, low, the music of it returning. "Despite my request to the contrary." One diamond eye winked. "We succeeded?"

I hugged his muzzle, leaning against him while he sighed deeply. "Always," I said. "We're unstoppable."

"You know now what you wear?" He'd known all along, hadn't he? And not told me. I stroked the black ribbon and remembered the beloved face I'd seen in the veil.

His face.

"I do," I said. "No wonder I could trust him. He's you."

Max sighed again. "I will always be there for you," he whispered, voice fading as his eye closed and he drifted into sleep. "No matter from which Universe."

The ribbon flexed and fell still, in agreement.

How lucky was this girl? So lucky. I hugged Max long after he'd gone to sleep and cried in relief he was still with me.

THIRTY-SIX

Weird to be living back at the house again. And yet, it was like full circle in many ways. I'd taken my old bedroom from when I was a teenager, deposing my daughter who wasn't here full time anyway. I missed seeing her, hugging her, my chance to talk to her privately gone. Dad had come when I was at the Stronghold, taken her to Harvard. She'd be safe, if more angry than ever, protected behind the walls of the NAWC. I'd see her tomorrow, once I had some sleep and a chance to process everything.

Yeah, bad mom. But I didn't think she needed this kind of mother in her life right now. One that couldn't get a wink without starting awake with a scream on her lips and Dark Brother's weighty shadow haunting her.

My bed called, pulled me in, hugged me tight. And sleep came easily and quickly.

The armor is heavy on my shoulders but I barely feel it, the pressure of building power pushing against me, burning through the metal and scorching my skin. I scream in defiance, using a voice already parched and cracking, and magic pulsing with the need to reach them before it's too late. The glowing, white sword of light hangs over my head, clenched in my gauntlet, lighting the savage spines of the dragon beneath me, his massive head arching backward, fire spouting in a cascade of heat and ash blowing past my cheek. My helmet is gone, I don't know where, but it doesn't matter. We're almost there, the building juggernaut of destructive force between the armies hurtling toward each other narrowing by the instant.

We soar into the barest crack that remains, the bellow of my companion the trigger for the power that bursts from us, the sword over my head erupting into a massive outward explosion of white sorcery that devours everything. Peace engulfs me as I die in the crushing press of the violent clash of their magic and mine.

I woke standing next to my bed, arm over my head, a hoarse shout dying in the back of my throat before it emerged. The house felt quiet, contained. So my little nightmare hadn't stirred anyone up. A wonder I hadn't wrecked the place. Talk about intense. And terrifying.

Why then did I feel calm all of a sudden? My arm fell to my side, the cold sweat on my upper lip drying as I shook myself and slowed my breathing on purpose.

So, that was how it would end. For once, I had answers. Good to know, oddly. Maybe I should tell Max we'd die together. He'd like that.

Unable to free myself from the morbid thought, I left my room and descended the stairs.

The backyard beckoned as it often did. I found myself in the quiet darkness of late fall, perched on the bench against the house, bare feet not feeling the cold as I sat crossed legged and stared up into the endless stars. At least they still seemed endless. I knew better.

Syd. Stop thinking. Just breathe.

Right. The meditation technique I'd been taught years ago at the insistence of my martial arts teacher had never quite served me, but now seemed a good idea to try to put it to use. Sage had often teased me about the unrest in my mind. He had no idea just how messy it was in here.

Case in point. Even as I inhaled, settling my hands on my knees, Quaid's face popped into my head and I suppressed a sigh. Whoever came up with the idea of meditation was either not in possession of any kind of stress or had more will power than I did. My brain was just too full of stuff.

You could say that again. My demon snorted and I hugged her despite her crankiness. She and the other girls had been so quiet since we escaped. I knew they were facing their own darkness and struggles with what we'd endured. We'd figure it out and cry on each other once the time was right. For now it was good just to hear her voice and know she was still with me.

Naturally, Shaylee whispered.

Always, my vampire sent.

I closed my eyes and counted my breath. In. Out. In. Out. Quaid. Damn it, there he was again. I hadn't seen him yet, since I got back. But being here in the back yard brought up so many memories of him it was hard to shove him aside.

And then Liam, naturally. I reached out, knowing he was gone, feeling for anything remotely Sidhe that wasn't Shaylee. Brushed over Galleytrot and Erica, both with Mom at Harvard. But absent their earth magic, just white sorcery calling to mine. And that was it.

No Liam. Like always.

Silly Syd.

Finally the dream. The battle on dragon back. The end.

The back door opened just as I sighed, knowing my feeble attempt at Zen anything was a lost cause. Sage would be ashamed of me. I looked up and into gray eyes, my stomach tightening at the sight of Oliver standing there in the bright light.

He'd changed out of his imposing armor and into jeans and a t-shirt. So weird seeing him looking normal all of a sudden, so easy to file into a brand new category of just another guy I knew. Nice to know the metal wasn't just for show, though. Muscles bunched and moved under his clothes as he raised one big hand and offered a wave, hesitant. Probably expecting me to shoo him off.

Just another guy? Yeah, delusional was my middle name.

I was going to ask him to leave but didn't, instead beckoning him to join me. Not like peace and quiet were getting me anywhere. He sat next to me, the wood bench flexing under his weight, broad jaw and high cheekbones starkly outlined by the backlight over the door.

"Sorry to interrupt," he said, voice quiet. "You were looking for something?"

I shook my head as I realized he felt my magical exploration, the hunt for Liam I might never, ever give up. Well, until I died with Max in the final battle. Downer. "Something long gone that I know better than to hope for." Double downer. I looked away, hugging myself. "I never did thank you for saving my life."

One of his hands rose, pushed hair away from his face. "You're welcome," he said.

When his arm fell I caught a faint scent from the motion, the breath of air stirred washing over and through me with a thrill of something I hadn't felt in a long time. The mix of earthiness and fabric softener.

No. It couldn't be. I found myself studying his face, heart pounding in my chest. Oliver must have sensed my change in mood because he tensed and met my gaze with his own gray eyes, leaning forward and blocking the light behind him. His silhouette, his outline, his scent…

Oh. My. Liam.

But no, not Liam. There was no Sidhe magic, no deep roots, no oak tree. Yes, there was power, tons of it, but foreign to me even as the white sorcery was now mundane.

Wishful thinking. And triggered one last truth, the final straw to break this camel's weary spine. There was no way Liam could have existed in the other Universe, I realized then with tears leaping to my eyes. There was no Sidhe magic there, no Gates, no Gatekeepers. No Cian and Aoilainn, no realm.

No O'Danes.

I wept without meaning to, breaking down in that instant of understanding, my hands over my face as if I could hold myself together with sheer physical strength. A part of me had clung to the thought maybe, just maybe, Liam was there, like Mia was there. That he'd survived and was happy, with a wife and kids and a normal life. Without me but alive and well. Despite me.

The truth was a hammer blow to my very soul.

His arms encircled me without hesitation, Oliver drawing me against his chest. I should have fought him, fought the tender way he stroked my hair, his cheek pressed to the top of my head, the way the heat of his body warmed me when grief offered only chill. But I needed comfort and he was there without judgment or expectation in his power. Forget this stirring of something I refused to acknowledge or permit to grow. Never would I allow another man in my heart. This was just sheer need of another warm body to lean on, nothing more.

Nothing. More.

And like I would ever have feelings for some random enemy dude who saved my ass and gave up everything to protect me.

Damn it, Syd. Just stop it.

You do realize, my vampire sent, *he's likely part of the reason we had to go…and perhaps for reasons your heart isn't willing to accept just yet.*

Shut up.

I finally pulled away, wiping my nose on the shoulder of my t-shirt, sighing out the last of my sadness as I sagged in place.

Rather than make a deal about it—smart man—Oliver sat quietly next to me with his hands folded in his lap. "I worry still what my presence here might mean."

Bless him for changing the damned subject. "Gabriel said you're good," I said. "So you're good." Because Gabriel and the Gateway and stuff.

Sigh.

"If I can help," he said. Hesitated. "I'm here, Syd. Fate must have a plan for me?" That last came out as a question. And empathy woke in me at last.

I reached over and took his hand in mine. "You know," I said, "we still have two pieces of Creator to find." Don't remind me. "And a Universe or two to collapse." Go Doombringer. "I'm sure you'll find something to do."

He chuckled. "I'm sure."

I liked his laugh. Ack.

Yes, I had a lot left to accomplish and a way to go. But I just needed a minute in my back yard in the quiet, holding his kind hand and staring at the stars.

Just one minute.

Turned out the Universe was okay with that.

THIRTY-SEVEN

I'm always amazed at the resilience of the people I care about—including me.

First, the bad news. There was nothing from Charlotte and Danilo about the Russian mafia. Mind you, with those two it was possible no news was actually good news, so I just let trust lead the way and hope they would find something we could use to help Femke.

Who, unfortunately, was back to being her crackpot self. Considering I now knew her soul was slowly dying off thanks to the invading chunk of Konstantin devouring her from the inside out, I at least understood what was happening. Doing something about it? Another matter entirely. Quaid was still working his magic to keep her together, a fact that increased my respect for my ex.

Weird that the half-crazed WPC leader was so protective of the Hensley sisters, though. Mom had managed to diffuse that situation when I was on the other side, convincing enough of the other world leaders that Tallah had stepped over the line. So, for the most part, the two Hensleys were at the mercy of Femke and her slowly devolving personality.

Well, they could have each other for now.

Piers had kindly waited to execute Jean Marc until I got back, bless his heart. The trial was going to be fantastic and I had a front row seat. Seriously though, while a side of me (I'm looking at you, demon) was thrilled by the opportunity, for the most part (thank you, vampire) I just wanted it to be over.

Leave it to my British friend to throw around terms like "legal" and "justice". Like the Dumont family had ever given one sweet crap about anything to do with fairness and the law.

Whatever.

Still, I had to admit it was fun the morning Piers and I stood outside Jean Marc's cell in Scotland and good naturedly argued over which of us got to kill him and exactly how we were going to do it. So there was that upside.

Two of the pieces of Creator—the eyes and the soul, whatever that meant—were still missing and, I feared, under the control of Belaisle. At least now I knew for 100% certain I could trust Trill. Maybe. Okay, hopefully. Ah, crap. As far as Fate allowed.

I'd take it.

I just wished I didn't have to stay so far in the dark where information was concerned. There was that term again. I couldn't avoid the black if I tried. And I tried.

There was no sign still of the maji, no word from Iepa and even Bellanca and Thanos were quiet. I wished I knew what the disappearance of the second race meant, though part of me refused to care about them. They'd done everything they could not to give a crap about us, hadn't they? So, if Bellanca lied and they were trapped in the void too, so be it. I guess I'd be forced to save them or be their doom along with everyone else when the time came.

If not? Well, I'd like to know where to go to run and hide. Because at this point it felt like a great option.

Who was I kidding? My mother raised me too well. I was in this for the long haul and if I had to destroy everything to do it, I'd own that whole Doombringer label, hell yeah.

Bring it.

My attempts to communicate directly with the black ribbon had failed so far, as though Max's alternate's soul wasn't able to speak to me. Or chose not to. Either way, I missed my big drach friend and would have appreciated some facetime with his Dark Universe twin just to make myself feel less guilty about what happened.

My one visit to the vampire mansion made me so sad

I vowed not to return until this was over. All the spirit power was gone and with Ameline missing from the maji chamber, there seemed to be no reason to go back anyway.

Something about standing in the giant, echoing foyer made me want to cry.

While there was no sign of the Order crossing into our Universe, the very thought of Dark Brother coming here made sleep impossible most nights. Any illusions I'd had about handling him or his army—the drachmor included—were long dead and gone, turned to dust, swept out the door with my hopes and dreams. Okay, dramatic much? But if they did burst that dam and come here... We were screwed, so screwed.

Couldn't go there.

Being in the veil itself felt immensely painful, the shrinking of the planes so obvious now it hurt just to pass through on my way places. I'd have to find a way to shield myself from it or suck it up and suffer along with the rubber membrane. To be fair, I didn't blame it for reaching for me and seeking its own brand of comfort when I rode through it, but I wished it would just keep its hurt to itself.

I was trying, damn it.

So, I said bad news first. That means there was good news, too. Max was recovering, thanks to the Stronghold's attention and that of his people. Mabel admitted concern and confusion as to why his wings weren't growing back as well as she'd hoped, but he seemed calm and peaceful when I visited. There was something different about him, a retreat in him I'd never felt before, probably tied to the fact the stubs over his shoulders seemed to be healing over instead of growing new tissue. Or so it looked to me. But who was I to judge drach healing methods or the enthusiasm of the Stronghold? Of course he'd been through a horrible trauma, so his quiet was fair enough, honestly. Time would tell if his reserved solitude would pass.

I could only hope it was temporary. I really needed him, now more than ever. Wings or no wings. Wince.

It was nice to see Piers elected the new leader of the combined sorcerers now that everything had reset to what Gabriel called normal. With the freshening of the Universe's sorcery, the release of all ties to affiliations, with no need for sorcery to be linked to one faction or another, things had calmed down a great deal. I wasn't the least surprised when Piers was chosen to head up the new, if loose, collection of sorcerers. Nor that he asked Demetrius to be his second. They were still working on a name that unified all sorcerers and their ranks kept growing, oddly, even as the other magical races vanished. Considering sorcery was the first power—and that the white version was spreading like wildfire, as it should—I guess I shouldn't have been surprised to see them holding their own.

Time would tell what that meant, exactly. And if they would be any match for Dark Brother and his peeps when the moment of truth came. Or if I just had to ruin everything and no one got to win.

Pessimist.

I'd hoped maybe with the collapse of the sorcerous ties Femke might snap out of her struggle, but it wasn't the power that was the trouble, it was the soul itself corrupting her. I assumed the Black Souls who Charlotte and Danilo pursued would have had their own affiliations severed. But would they simply work together anyway, old habits and all that? Likely. Just because they were no longer linked the way they had been didn't mean they were suddenly nice guys.

Sorry, back to the good news.

Lovely to see Sass and Jiao were now inseparable. I wondered how deeply her faked betrayal had hurt the young *lóng*. We hadn't yet had a chance to debrief, both needing time to process. She clung to my demon friend and had no problems showing her affection publically, much to his delight (and frequent blushing). And nice for her, her people who had once been enslaved to Moa now lived at the Stronghold. Sass was home less and less frequently and I hardly blamed him, though I missed his company and comfort.

He'd earned his own happily ever after, no matter

how long it lasted.

Jeeze, stop with the doom and gloom already. Doombringer must refer to being a grouchy pants.

The Hensley coven members had all been relocated and the territory assigned to a new family, according to Mom. They'd gone quietly, unlike their leader and her sister, even the werewolves who'd once been part of that family meekly accepting the change. Of course, Mom wasn't having it completely easy, but at least her territory was whole again.

Wins all around.

Varity continued to impress me, standing firm at Mom's side and being exactly the kind of Enforcer Leader my mother needed. Partially thanks to the white sorcery she now commanded like a pro, and partially because Quaid was on our side. Still, I was grateful knowing the old witch—two looming, black hounds part of the deal—had my mother's back.

The Zornov family, minus Trill of course, had appeared back in Wilding Springs while I was gone. Nice to see Nona's trailer in the driveway at the house. Even more so the fact Simon joined them. He didn't exactly sneak back in, but nothing was said about how he left and I let him have his simple, quiet return. It was good to have the gang back again.

As way of apology, the young hacker managed to double the family fortune, to Gram's shock. I took it as the sorry it was and wondered how much of the money he'd spend himself in the next little while on new gadgets. There was lots to go around.

And now, the subject I'd been avoiding while wondering what the hell to do with him. Naturally, my daughter hated Oliver from the moment they met. Didn't help the Order soldier saw past her batting eyelashes and manipulative ways and called her on them with a smirk on his face. Yeah, that won her over. Not.

Quaid wasn't a fan either, though he said it was because he didn't think we could trust Oliver. Well, he had a point about the whole mortal enemy thing. Except that nothing was further from the truth. Whatever. I let my ex have his macho bullying only because it made Oliver grin and push back.

Snort.

The family was on the fence too, Gram eyeing him when she thought I wasn't looking. Which wasn't often. It seemed every time I turned around I almost ran into him. Without asking, without anyone even talking it over, he'd moved into the downstairs bedroom Gram used to use. Whether Gram didn't protest because she thought I'd suggested it to him or she'd made the offer without telling me, Oliver just sort of became part of our lives. My lurking shadow, gray eyes following me everywhere even when his body didn't. And I fought with myself constantly over the fact I didn't make him stop.

He was the enemy. He had information that could help us. I hoped. That was all this was. And Oliver had been open and willing to answer any questions I had so far. I just hoped that didn't change when the rest of the Universe fell apart or if he was faced with an "us or them" situation.

At least Gabriel seemed to trust him completely, even openly adored him, a fact not lost on Ethie or Quaid. Probably made things worse.

Who was I kidding? Probably? Might as well pour hot oil on a fire and call it a solution.

Didn't matter I agreed with my son. Or the fact every passing moment I grew more accustomed to having Oliver by my side. That it quickly became comfortable to find him watching me. If I had to be totally truthful with myself, my heart didn't matter.

Nothing did. Maybe later, maybe after this was done I could think about what my life might look like. But not now.

The Universe needed me. Creator needed me. And I'd be damned if I was going to let them down.

Oliver. Sigh.

He had to have beautiful eyes, didn't he?

Like what you read? Find out more at
pattilarsen.com

Here's a look at the first chapter of
Book Seven of the Hayle Coven Destinies

DARK BROTHER

ONE

Jean Marc Dumont's trial should have felt like a giant victory. Why then did I feel like such a grouch sitting on the hard, stone chair I'd been assigned, glaring around me with my arms crossed over my chest at anyone who even hinted at intruding on my bad mood?

Four days. Four freaking days since my return from the Dark Universe, since my mind and body and soul were torn apart by Creator's sibling, Her heart putting me back together again. Four days since Max's wings were sliced from his drach body, any attempt at regrowth with help from his people and the newly restored Stronghold failing. Four days since a giant chunk of the Universe fell through the crumbling veil and into the void.

And what had I done since returning with a bit of knowledge about the other side and a massive, hulking, metal clad soldier of the Order in tow? Nada. Ziperino. El Zilcho.

Because now freaking what?

Not a sniff of the other two pieces made it to my son. Gabriel was our only line to the missing chunks of Creator's statue and he'd run up against a blank wall that might as well have been a hell no from the Universe itself. Just thinking about the delay made me want to hurt someone. We'd come so far, only to be stymied in the past. Then, in liquid fast time, four pieces were located and returned. All within the agenda Fate laid out.

Gabriel told me we were in a race against time at this point. So, if that was true, why were we again sitting on our hands, twiddling our thumbs at each other while the veil fell apart and people vanished into the black nothing?

Because, that's why. Because. And that was the best answer I was getting from anyone who would talk to me. Mom just shrugged, darkness under her eyes growing deeper by the day. She had her own mess with the NAWC and the fact the other world territories didn't like her plan to make her council all coven inclusive. They could suck it as far as I was concerned. Piers wasn't much help, the whole renewal of sorcery keeping him busy. He'd been named the leader of all sorcerers for some reason and with Demetrius Strong at his side as his second, he wasn't wasting time taking over the world.

And Jiao's apparent betrayal in the other Universe

turned intel gathering mission hadn't given me anything I didn't already know, much to her disappointment. The drachmor jerkfaces would have their punishment, would they ever. They'd pay for what they did to Max, the cowards. Running off like they did to the Dark Universe, abandoning ours. Fate or not, respect wasn't due and I refused to even consider cutting slack. But, it had to hurt Jiao, the fact her turning on me to save me had led her to nothing I didn't uncover myself.

Ack. I really needed a better attitude. At least someone was seeing progress, case in point as the masses of sorcerers gathered in the room writhed with intense eagerness. And I couldn't think of anyone better to lead the new Sorcerers League than Piers Southway. Crabbypants I might have been, but I appreciated the fact someone I cared about was in power instead of some asshat who would ruin everything.

He'd been kind enough to offer the distraction of Jean Marc's trial, too. The trip to Scotland wasn't a happy one, though, and part of the reason for my terrible mood. Every time I rode the veil these days I couldn't help but feel its intense pain and sadness, feel the shrinkage of its former limitless potential. There were times it reached out to me like a hurt puppy and asked—not in so many words, mind you—for my help. Explaining to it I was doing my best wasn't going over very well. Try talking to the rubber membrane between the planes sometime in terms it will understand.

Yeah. Crash and burn.

I was big enough to admit my grumpiness was a shield to hide my fear. The frailty and fragility of the constant the veil had been for who knew how many centuries wasn't lost on me. Nor was the fact we were losing whole races and planes into the void, our fault as we rebuilt Creator's statue. And we couldn't stop now, could we? The end of everything was inevitable. Our only hope was to follow this order the new Fate of our Universe, Zoe Helios, and my friend turned betrayer turned I didn't know what yet, Trill Zornov, talked about.

Maybe if Trill and Zoe were on the same page. Instead, it seemed like the two were at odds. According to Trill—who I'd recently thought a traitor only to have her guide me to pieces she herself had stolen from me—Zoe was being influenced, that Fate herself was cheating.

Comforting thought. Especially when returning the pieces in order seemed so important. Gabriel stressed it too, even told me some of them had been replaced out of sync. And now I understood placing those pieces linked intrinsically to the very elemental magicks of the Universe, that with the right combination those powers disappeared into the void as they were supposed to. Was that even something I could accept? They were supposed to? How could Creator purposely have set us up to ruin everything?

Questions and more questions and growl, snort, grumble, grrr.

Whatever reason Zoe had for working for the other side remained a mystery. I couldn't find her, not in the Sanctuary where she'd once lived—where Jean Marc had been captured—nor here in Scotland with the man who loved her, or anywhere else, for that matter. I knew my enemy and the mouthpiece of Dark Brother in this Universe, Liander Belaisle, had his own stronghold somewhere, but the idea she could be working with him just didn't play out. Zoe wouldn't sell us out to Dark Brother. She was Creator's Fate. Whoever was manipulating her, she had to trust them.

I had a few horrible suspicions, but kept them to myself. Because I couldn't find those two, either. But I knew one thing for absolute certain. If Bellanca and Thanos—the original Fates—were involved in this, nothing would save them.

A tall, black haired woman collapsed into the stone seat beside me, letting out a loud gust of air. Scowling only made my sister's human form more beautiful, though I wasn't in the mood to tell her so. Meira, the Ruler of Demonicon and the one person in the Universe who wouldn't care if I was crabby to her, tapped her fingernails on the arm rest of her chair and glared back.

"You look happy," she snapped.

"Oh, shut up," I snarled.

Meira grinned suddenly, hands rising to make a nest of tentacles under her chin. "Thorry, Thyd," she said.

The image of her nickname for me flashed in my head, Syd the Squid actually prodding my funny bone and making me snort.

"How come no one knew you were such a horrible little girl?" I felt myself relax in her presence. I'd always loved my sister, of course I did. But as we got older—as the weight of the Universe settled on us both—it seemed we had only grown closer. With the exception of her fury with me at running away for six months, I think even that had strengthened our bond. I didn't think of her as my baby sis anymore, my Meems. She was Meira, one of my best friends. An equal who understood with more clarity than anyone else in my life just what being me was like.

"Because," she said with a wink of one blue eye, her natural amber showing through her magic for a moment in a flare of demon fire, "they were always so focused on what a jerk you were. Made my job easy."

Fair enough. I reached over and squeezed her hand when it fell back to her armrest. *How are things?*

She shrugged mentally, but her power felt diminished as she let me in, the giant, vast reserve of Demonicon in her possession feeling hollow, echoing. *How do you think?*

I winced and looked away. *I'm sorry, Meems.*

If I thought it was your fault, she sent, *I'd accept that apology.* She sighed in my head. *I should be more afraid, shouldn't I? My entire power base is collapsing, disappearing. The Node that holds my planes together burbles happily despite the fact it's falling to pieces while the spirit of our dead grandmother tells me over and over I'm worried about nothing. My people are vanishing into thin air along with their domains. And I'm here, at a trial for a former Dumont I really don't give a crap about anymore.*

She was right. I realized it as I sat there, inhaling the mildly damp air of the Scottish castle. Where once I'd hated Jean Marc and his family, despised everything they stood for, they didn't seem important any longer. With Andre's death thanks to my werefriend Charlotte's magic curse, the Dumont family power had died with him, leaving his two sons and their coven to fend for themselves. Whatever became of Kristophe I had no idea. At least he had turned out to be a weak and unthreatening witch who didn't seem all that eager to follow in Daddy's evil footsteps. As for Jean Marc, his possession of the once rare white sorcery had given him an edge over the former Steam Union, gave him leadership of the now defunct Brotherhood. And removed him about as far from my radar as anyone.

I really should have just gone, gotten up and left. Piers could handle this. But even as the thought crossed my mind, the main doors to the chamber opened and my tall, blond friend entered, the Dumont eldest in chains behind him.

Trapped. I sagged, shrugged to my sister. *At least this*

will be quick.

She sighed and nodded.

Priorities. Funny how much they changed when the Universe was dying.

ABOUT THE AUTHOR

Everything you need to know about me is in this one statement: I've wanted to be a writer since I was a little girl, and now I'm doing it. How cool is that, being able to follow your dream and make it reality? I've tried everything from university to college, graduating the second with a journalism diploma (I sucked at telling real stories), am part of an all-girl improv troupe (if you've never tried it, I highly recommend making things up as you go along as often as possible). I've even been in a Celtic girl band (some of our stuff is on YouTube!) and was an independent film maker. My life has been one creative thing after another—all leading me here, to writing books for a living.

Now with multiple series in happy publication, I live on beautiful and magical Prince Edward Island (I know you've heard of Anne of Green Gables) with my very patient husband and multitude of pets.

I love-love-love hearing from you! You can reach me (and I promise I'll message back) at patti@pattilarsen.com. And if you're eager for your next dose of Patti Larsen books (usually about one release a month) come join my mailing list! All the best up and coming, giveaways, contests and, of course, my observations on the world (aren't you just dying to know what I think about everything?) all in one place: http://smarturl.it/PattiLarsenEmail.

Last—but not least!—I hope you enjoyed what you read! Your happiness is my happiness. And I'd love to hear just what you thought. A review where you found this book would mean the world to me—reviews feed writers more than you will ever know. So, loved it (or not so much), **your honest review would make my day**. Thank you!